Because of Us

BECAUSE OF LOVE SERIES 0.5

DEVON MAY

Because of Us
Copyright © 2024 by Devon May

All rights reserved. Without limiting the rights under copyright reserved above, no part of this publication may be reproduced, stored in or introduced into retrieval system, or transmitted, in any form, or by any means (electronic, mechanical, photocopying, recording, or otherwise) without the prior written permission of both the copyright owner and the above publisher of this book.

This is a work of fiction. Names, characters, places, brands, media, and incidents are either the products of the author's imagination or are used fictitiously. The author acknowledges the trademarked status and trademark owners of various products referenced in this work of fiction, which have been used without permission. The publication/use of these trademarks is not authorized, associated with, or sponsored by the trademark owners.

Edited by: Ashleigh Van Arkkels at AVA Book Editing
Cover Design: Books and Moods
Formatted by: Stacey at Champagne Book Design

Books by

DEVON MAY

BECAUSE OF LOVE SERIES
Because of Us (novella)
Because of Her (April 2024)
Because of Them (late 2024)

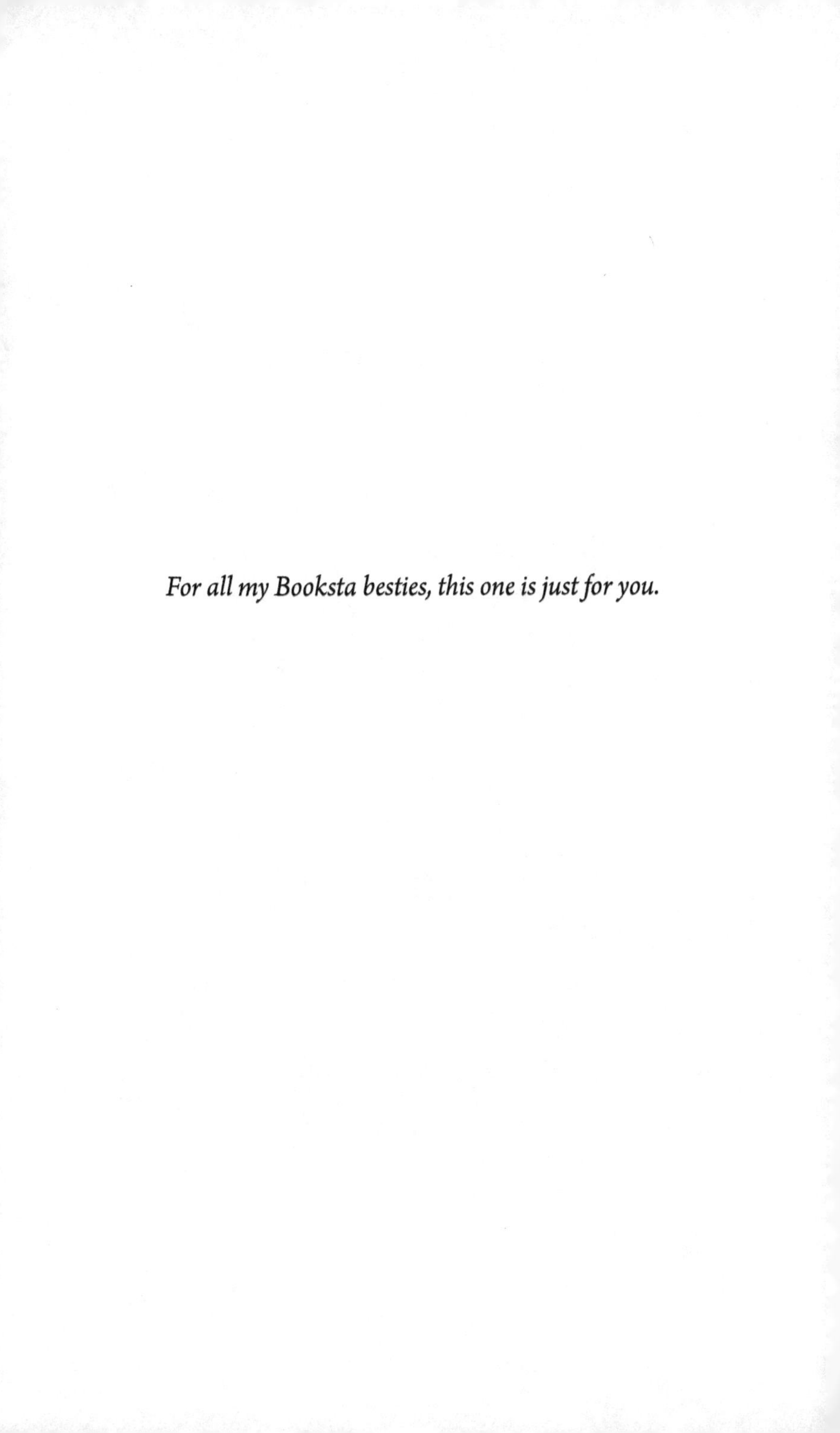

For all my Booksta besties, this one is just for you.

Author's Note

The Because of Love series is a steamy contemporary romance set in Melbourne, Australia. To stay true to the characters and the author, it is written in Australian English. There may be times you spot a *u* where you weren't expecting one, or an *s* instead of a *z*. It is my hope that you are so invested in Oliver and Madison's story that you don't notice them.

Trigger Warning: *Because of Us* is a story of finding love in the places you shouldn't. It includes sexual content between two consenting adults. One is a professor; the other is his student. If this is potentially triggering for you, please read on with care.

Because of Us

Chapter One

MADISON

Alone. For the first time in my life, I'm going to be alone.

Tears stream down my face as I'm forced to say goodbye to the only person I could ever truly rely on. Hidden in this small corner of the library, no one can see my meltdown, but it's only a matter of time before someone strolls past.

"I thought you weren't leaving until next month?"

Cassidy makes a popping sound with her mouth. The sound reverberates through the phone line, clicking painfully in my ear.

"So did I." She sighs. "Blake's work wants him to start earlier."

"Can he not go now, and you can go later?"

"I wish I could, but he is driving the car. I can't let him tackle the drive alone, it's too far."

I can't help but feel hurt. The drive to Sydney isn't *that* far. I wanted my sister to see me off on my first official day here at Melbourne University. Now she won't be able to, I'm reminded of why I don't trust easily.

People have a way of letting me down.

"I have to go." Cassidy's voice is tender, but I hear it start to crack. "I'll be at dad's lunch tomorrow, at least."

Hanging up the phone, I let the tears fall.

I forgot we had planned lunch with our father. We don't do it as often as we probably should, but it's always so draining when we do. Judgement swirls in his eyes when he asks if I'm seeing someone. It bores into me until my insides turn to stone under the crushing weight of his expectations. Disappointment laces his words every time I tell him that no, I don't think I'll see the guy from last weekend again.

He always wants more from me. Expects more from me. He has never understood that I'm not like Cassidy, and I doubt he will start now. I don't want to settle down. I don't want to put that much trust in another person. I don't think I can. My mother's swift departure to a new man—a new family—when I was barely a teenager sliced a wound too wide, too deep.

Maybe I could feign illness just so I won't have to put up with his incessant questions. I would, if tomorrow's lunch wasn't also the last time I'll see my sister before she leaves.

She always helps to deflect the questions, turning the attention back on herself and her perfect life. Leaving me to calm the storm in my mind and refocus my thoughts.

One more lunch. That's all I have left with my sister before she leaves me to deal with our father alone. It's not his fault, I'm sure it's only natural for a father to want the best for his daughters. I know he means well, but it's exhausting.

Throwing my phone back in my bag, I search for a tissue. I hate that I'm so worked up over this. Families move around all the time, it's not like Cass is leaving forever. Not like our mother did. Not like all the boys I've ever loved did.

I can't help comparing her to them though.

Finding plenty of hair ties, but no tissue, I give up the search through my bag and tug at the sleeves of my cotton dress. The grey fabric goes dark as I reach under my glasses to wipe at my tears.

Bit by bit, I start to compose myself. When my breaths steady, I open the book in my lap. On any other day my nose would be deep inside a fluffy romance novel. Stephen King's memoir looks about as far from that as possible. But it was listed as recommended reading for the Creative Non-Fiction class I added to my schedule and, me being me, I have to read it.

I bought all the other books on the list. After two years of trying, and failing, to become a successful writer, I finally realised I needed to learn more about the craft. Somehow, my meagre attempts at writing best-selling novels caught the attention of faculty and I was offered a creative writing scholarship. There are no promises that anything they can teach me will guarantee success, but this is my last chance to achieve my dream. If I don't find success as an author soon, I'll need to find some other way to support myself. I can't live off my barista salary forever.

The problem is that more than half of the

recommended texts have such outdated advice that I want to tear them up and use them for craft purposes. Maybe fold all the pages to spell out a word. At least then they could look pretty, even if they aren't useful. *On Writing* was added at the last minute, along with the change in professor. With such little notice, I decided to try borrowing it to see if it was worth actually buying this one.

Flicking through the pages, I'm not *really* paying attention. I know I'll have to read it again later. Some time when I'm not feeling so brain dead. When the words don't jumble around so much, and the sentences make sense. When I can focus on what I'm reading instead of hyper-fixating on the emotion that is drowning me. For now, though, reading is a mild distraction from the pain in my chest. This is what Cassidy was warning me about, all those years ago, and every year since.

"I love you sissy," she used to say, "but I can't be your only friend. You have to trust other people."

It was easy for her to say. She had her best friend. Her and Callum were joined at the hip … until they weren't. But even then, she always managed to find her place with the people she works with. And then she met Blake, and everything just clicked for her.

I wish I could have that, but every time I let someone in, they let me down. It started with my mother and then everyone else seemed to follow suit. No one gets me the way Cassidy does. I don't think anybody ever will.

Pushing myself to stand, I tuck my hair behind my ears and push my shoulders back.

The library is quiet as I meander my way back to the entrance, still trying to focus on the words I'm reading instead of my feelings. Aisles of bookshelves in between empty rows wave me goodbye as I glance up from the book. Everyone has left and a hint of panic hits me. I scurry between the shelves towards the exit, panic fuelling my legs as I worry they might have closed the library. The corner where I had sat to cry was at the furthest end of the space, away from the librarian's desk and the countless communal desks. They easily could have missed me on a final sweep. Approaching the open space near the entrance I rush my way around the corner at the end of the aisle.

The book, still open under my nose, hits my face. It squishes my glasses into the bridge of my nose. The force of the collision throws me to the ground, and I land firmly on my ass. My dress is bunched around my waist, and the sting from my nose threatens to make my eyes well up all over again.

Pushing my glasses up, I press my hands against my eyes. I try, in vain, to hold the tears in.

"Shit!"

The deep husky voice shocks me. Heat rises up my neck when I realise I'm not alone. My chest tightens as I race to pull my dress over my legs. The fabric that fell to my knees when I was standing feels too short, barely covering my thighs in this position.

I glance up at the man and feel instant regret. He is older than me, more refined. But not too far older that I don't still find him beyond attractive. The fabric of his suit pants stretches over his thighs as he crouches down. One hand still clutching at the hemline of my dress, I hesitate before stretching the other toward him.

Instead of helping me, he jumps back up. The abruptness of his movements has me pulling back my hand to clutch at my stomach. My heart flops when I see the sultry glare in his deep brown eyes.

Noticing the rest of his face, my hands fly up to cover my face again. A hint of stubble is starting to show around his jaw, highlighting the gentle shape of his lips. The man is so attractive I want to melt in his presence. I want the floor to swallow me whole because I don't think I'll ever get over the embarrassment. When the floor holds its place underneath me, I sob.

I sob because I thought today couldn't get any worse. Because I just wanted to get home. Because everything hurts. My heart, my nose, my ass. My pride.

Chapter Two

OLIVER

The library is empty by the time I close my computer. The few students that had come to make a start on their weekly readings have all left. Off to orientation week activities and wild parties.

I remember those days well. Back when I thought I knew what I wanted out of life. When I thought my work here would mean something. But those days are long gone, and all the years I spent working on my doctorate feel wasted.

Everyone knows the saying, those that can't do, teach. Except that, I can do. My writing has won awards. My books have sold millions of copies around the world. I just chose to teach anyway. I thought I could make a difference in the lives of young creatives. Inspire them to write their stories, to sell their stories.

If my years as a postgraduate tutor taught me anything, I doubt I'll be instilling motivation in anyone this semester. Turns out, most of the students that take Creative Non-Fiction are only in it because they have to be. Or because they need extra credit points and figure it'll be an easy slide.

Honestly, those ones are right. There's nothing compelling for me to teach them, no big 'ah-ha' moment. At least, nothing that will help them write a best-selling book. That shit is all hard work, little reward.

Dreading the start of semester next week, my thoughts shift to the money that landed in my bank account last month. I don't want it. I certainly don't deserve it.

Nobody holds a lottery ticket expecting to win, but somehow, I did. I won.

And I still haven't spent a dime. It doesn't feel real, but it also doesn't feel right. The ticket was a cheap addition to a Christmas Hamper I won in a raffle. I nearly threw it out. But then I heard on the news about the unclaimed winnings. My jaw dropped when I checked the numbers.

Ten. Million. Dollars.

I don't need it, and I'm sure there are far less fortunate people who do. I just need to find the best way to get it to them.

I gather my belongings from the desk, giving up my attempts to write a lecture plan for next week. Sliding my laptop into my satchel and stacking the books, I pick everything up. My mind is elsewhere as I trudge down the hall between aisles on my way out. The stack of books is unbalanced in my arms, teetering just like my desire to work at the university.

She hits me with full force, knocking the wind out of my lungs, and the ground from beneath her feet. Flying backwards, the petite blonde woman lands firmly on her ass while I lose my grip on the pile of books.

"Shit!"

I crouch down to pick up the books, before jumping upright. I'll get them later. Right now, I need to distract my gaze away from the woman's black lace panties.

I can't … shouldn't … won't … look. No matter how much I want to. But then I hear her sob.

The sound does something weird to my insides. They twist in an unusual way, leaving my chest feeling hollow.

I drop to my knees in front of her, thankful that she has done what little she can to pull her dress down. The vision of her dress bunched around her waist is burned into my mind. I fight to hold back the incredibly inappropriate desire to plant my face between her legs.

The woman is crying for God's sake.

I shake my head, running my hands through my hair in a desperate attempt to compose myself.

"Are you okay?"

Her hands inch away from her face, causing her glasses to fall into place over her nose. My hands twitch, wanting to reach out to her. Red bruising lines the bridge of her nose and her eyes are swollen. Puffy from what looks like hours of crying, not just the collision.

Seeing me reaching for her, she hiccups, shaking her head before hiding in her hands again.

"Please leave," she whispers into her hands.

My heart does that weird twisty thing again and I know that I can't leave her like this. I wouldn't leave anyone on the floor like this, but there is something about this woman that calls to me. Like we are tied together by an increasingly shortening rope.

I shake my head.

"It goes against my very nature to walk away from a person who so clearly needs help."

Her whole body slouches as I adjust my weight to sit down beside her. But she doesn't crawl away.

"I'm Oliver."

She sniffs before answering. "Madison."

Her voice is raspy, whether by nature or due to the crying I don't know, but it melodies in my ears. I want to hear her talk more. About anything. About everything.

"So, are you okay?" I repeat the question even though I'm not fully expecting her to answer.

Her shoulders shrug, but she pulls her hands from her face, wiping her eyes on her grey sleeves as she does. She is stunning. Blonde hair falls in gentle waves past her shoulders, and even with the bruising and puffiness, she is perfect.

"Not really."

Her answer hits my chest like a hammer, the urge to make everything okay surging through me. Unexpected anger courses through my veins, my blood boiling that someone has caused this much hurt. This woman, Madison, is drawing every emotion possible out of me. Emotions I haven't experienced in a long time. It's concerning, but somehow endearing. I need to find out why my body has such a strange reaction to her. But first I need to help her stop crying. With each tear the hammer drives a nail deeper into my heart. I can't stand her tears.

I push my boots into the carpet as the wave of emotion recedes.

"Do you … want to talk about it?"

For a second, she stares up at me. Her eyes blank as she blinks away tears. She closes them, shaking her head before answering.

"You know what, sure." She sucks in a deep breath. "Everyone leaves. Everyone lets me down. I have only ever had my sister, but now she is leaving too. The one person I could rely on. Gone. Just like all the others."

I have no idea how to respond. Instead, I stretch my arm around her, hovering my hand over her shoulder before finally settling it down. Her head falls to my shoulder. My pulse jumps as her hair settles down my back.

"Where is she going?"

"Sydney." Wincing, she turns to look up at me. "I mean, I have nothing against Sydney, but she is only going so that she can be with her boyfriend and it just … I don't know, it irks me that he is making her move."

"Did she not get a say?"

"No. I mean, maybe? She is a florist, so she can work anywhere. He wants to be a journalist, and apparently Sydney is the place to be. So, they made the decision to leave." Holding her hands up, she air quotes the word 'they'.

"I get the impression you don't like him?"

"What gave it away?"

She smiles. And everything else disappears. How much I hate my job, the all-consuming decision of what to do with the money, the books I left scattered on the floor. The library. Shit, the library. If she is a student …

Jerking my arm off her shoulders, I scramble away to collect the books lying around us. My rapid movement causes her to push to her feet. From my knees, I look up to see her holding my favourite book. It has to be a coincidence.

"What's wrong?" Madison raises an eyebrow as she takes in my frantic state.

Piling the last book into my arms, I stand to face her.

"Are you a—" My throat squeezes shut, the word refusing to come out even though it's crucial that I know the answer. I doubt it would put a stop to the confusing range of emotions still swirling through me.

I don't believe in love at first sight. I barely believe in lust at first sight. But there is no denying that there is something special about Madison. Something I can't look away from, pulling me towards her and holding me close.

"—a student?" The words finally force their way through my throat, and I choke as they do.

"Technically, not until next week."

One knife lodges itself in my throat. Another hits my chest, and a third finds home in my gut.

Every inappropriate thought from the past ten minutes gathers in my brain, forming a storm I have no hope of controlling. A single word leaps out, and I grasp hold of it. I shouldn't, but I do.

She isn't *technically* a student. Yet.

But I can live with yet. I have to live with yet. Because if I don't, I might crumble.

Madison doesn't ask if I'm a student too. I don't blame her. Although I'm young to be a professor, I'm visibly older than most students. The hair around my temples has a speckle of grey, and the smile lines around my eyes tend to stick.

I should ask her more, offer to get to know her. But I need to get us out of the library. Aside from the fact it will be closing soon, I can't risk any faculty members seeing us.

"Do you want to go get a drink?"

There's a glimmer in her crystal blue eyes this time she smiles. The corners of her eyes tilt up with her lips as she nods.

I'm glad the library is almost empty as we leave. No sneaky librarians poking their eyes around corners, spying on patrons. Madison stops to loan the book she won't put down, and I fight the urge to ask her why she needs it. I don't want to know.

At the campus bar, I choose a table for us in the back, angled away from the crowd that will no doubt begin to trickle in soon. We share a bowl of fries, and a pitcher of beer, and I can't help but feel cosy. At ease in a way I haven't in a long time. As though Madison's sheer presence is enough to make me forget all my worries.

All the worries that shouldn't feel so terrible but some-how do.

"So, what do you do?" She asks as I pour the last dregs of beer into her glass.

I suck in a breath, worrying my lips. I don't know what I should tell her. If I told her the truth, would she care? Before the pause drags too long, I blurt out an answer.

"I work at the university." A half-truth, not a lie. It feels like a lie though.

A smirk tugs at one corner of her mouth. Her eyes dart around the room before landing on mine.

"Are we allowed to be here? Together?"

My knee shakes under the table.

"Technically, only until next week."

Her gaze darkens as she inhales before letting the air out of her lungs in a deep sigh. Licking her lower lip as she leans forward on the table, her hands reach across for my own.

"We better make the most of it then."

Chapter Three

MADISON

The book on Oliver's bedside table screams at me. I don't want to think about what it means. I want to think about the man behind me. His hands roam over my body as he stirs awake, and I push my body closer to his.

I knock the book off the table. Tomorrow, I officially become a student. *His* student, if my suspicions are correct. I only have one day left with this man. I refuse to spend it thinking about the predicament we are sure to find ourselves in.

I'd only wanted one night. After we collided and I sobbed into his shoulder, Oliver showed me a kindness I would never have expected. His caring touch, his gentle voice, and the lust that filled his eyes ignited a spark inside me. I had to know what it would be like to let the fire spread.

But even after a whole week, I'm left craving more. Our bodies fit together in the most instinctual and lavish way. As though we were made for each other. The flame has engulfed us both, and feeling his nakedness against my own, I doubt I'll ever be able to put it out.

A rush of cool air hits me. Oliver pulls the blankets down, ducking low until he rests between my legs.

"Good morning." He stares up at me, a wicked grin across his face.

I squirm, kicking my legs at his shoulders. "I want breakfast."

"Me first."

His forearms find place over my thighs, holding me still while he drags his tongue up my core. Heat rushes through me, filling my belly. I rest back on the pillow, eyes rolling back in my head as he licks and sucks every inch of my pussy. His assault is relentless.

This. This is what I'll never get enough of.

A gasp escapes me as he inserts a finger, then two. They curl inside me, rubbing against that inner spot he knows drives me wild. My hips buck against him as heat rushes through me, building to something I can't control.

Teeth graze against my clit as he fucks me with his fingers.

"C'mon Mads, all over me." His growl drags me further into the blaze until it consumes me. Every muscle in my body constricts, a breathy moan hovering from my lips. Oliver pumps his fingers in and out, guiding me through my orgasm until every muscle in my body relaxes.

He grabs his cock, pumping it a few times. Rubbing his firm length through my lips, he coats it with the wetness that still pools between my legs. In one swift movement, Oliver flips me to my front and leans over my body to grab a condom from the drawer. Goosebumps erupt over me when he sits up to roll it on.

He slides into me from behind, pressing his body against my back. I'll never be done with feeling this full. I push my ass towards him, angling our bodies so his thrusts hit just right. Pounding back against him.

"Fuck." It's more of a moan than a word, and I can't be sure who utters it.

Reaching an arm around me, Oliver pulls me up to my knees. His other arm twists around my hair, pushing my upper half into the bed. My ass on display, he uses me for his pleasure, thrusting into me over and over and over. And I enjoy every moment of it. The fire starts to build again.

His fingers slide down to pinch my clit, and he leans down to kiss my neck.

"Such a good girl."

I come apart at his praise, right as Oliver pulls out of me. The condom snaps as he pulls it off, releasing himself in hot spurts across my back.

"Madison, you're perfect."

Firm fingers massage my ass, dipping between my legs to rub my wetness around my pussy. One trails up through his cum as he moans.

"I want to fill you with this one day."

A lump forms in my throat. We haven't discussed anything beyond this week, but God it sounds good. If only we didn't have such a finite end. Scooping me into his arms, Oliver carries me to the shower.

"It's closer to lunch time," he muses as we stand under the water.

"Pizza?"

Pulling me close, he nibbles my ear. "Perfect."

⁕

"I could walk here," I say with a mouth full of the most incredible pizza I've ever had.

"For someone who claims to love pizza as much as you do, I'm surprised you didn't know about it."

"And I'm surprised you've never had a barbeque chicken pizza, but here we are."

Oliver steals a slice from the box in front of me, eyeing it suspiciously before taking a bite.

"Not terrible."

He drove us here, but the pizzeria is closer to my apartment than his. A smoky, greasy, burnt cheese smell fills the space, no doubt coming from the woodfire oven taking pride of place through the kitchen doors. Wooden panels line the walls, and small bench seats take place at each of the tables.

I wish I'd known about this place sooner. I would have spent every weekend here. Maybe I would have met Oliver sooner and we could have had more time.

I drop the pizza, wiping my hand on a napkin before my head falls into my hands.

Oliver reaches an arm around my shoulder, sliding me along the seat. Our legs press together, and I lean into his touch. This is how we are supposed to be. My body has known it all week, but now that we are about to depart, I think my mind knows it too.

"Tomorrow," I start, but the end of the sentence won't come. It's too hard to say the words.

"I know. It's going to be shit."

I never wanted to fall into these feelings. I never expected them, for anybody. But of course, in my moment of weakness I went and fell headfirst. I've fallen for the man I can't have, and it's about to break my already fractured heart. Typical.

I take another bite of pizza for courage, counting each chew as I figure out the right words before I say them.

"I didn't want this. I wanted something fun and carefree and loose. But I think I found more than that. And I hate that we have to stop."

Staring down at my food, I blink away the tears. We met with me crying, I refuse to let that be how we end.

"What if you're my—"

"Don't say it." Oliver's hand tilts my chin until my eyes meet his. "I don't want to think about that. Whatever happens, it'll be okay. This week has been incredible, but it will be okay."

The corners of his lips drop, and I catch the hiccup in his words. He doesn't believe it any more than I do. But he is right, whatever happens, it has to be okay. We set a timer for our fun, and now the alarm is ringing.

Chapter Four

OLIVER

In front of me, the machine whirs to life, coffee dripping into the mug. I'm on my third cup this morning, and although my hands are starting to shake, I still feel exhausted.

We had a week, and it was a blissful one.

After the night in the bar, and the evening that followed it, Madison and I fell into step with each other. The boundaries were drawn so clearly, without either of us saying a word. We knew we had a week, and we knew not to ask questions. I don't know what she is studying, she doesn't know what I'm teaching.

Last night, our bodies wrapped around one another, we said goodbye. See you soon. This was fun.

It shouldn't have hurt the way it did, but I also should have known I had gone too far.

From the moment I saw Madison smile I knew I needed her. When I found out I couldn't truly have her, I selfishly took everything she had to give. One night with a forbidden love is one thing. A whole week is another. We were doomed from the start.

"Late night?"

The high-pitched voice startles me, but I manage to compose myself before turning around.

"Morning." I attempt a smile at the old crone, but her cold stare has my spine tingling.

Professor Heather Dausset runs a tight ship. Known for her strict staff expectations and no-nonsense attitude toward students, she is the head of the Creative Arts Faculty. My boss. And the woman who never wanted me working here in the first place.

According to her, I am too young to run such a 'crucial' class. My accolades as a writer meant nothing in her search for perfection. Lucky for me, no one else wanted to teach Creative Non-Fiction. Or unlucky, considering the foul taste that becoming a professor has left in my mouth. The thought of my first class sits like a frog in my stomach, bouncing around when I need it to be still. I became a professor to make a difference, but now that I'm part of the faculty, I'm doubting that's possible.

"Your first class starts in eight minutes."

I hold back a sarcastic remark. It won't do me any favours.

"Yes, thank you, I was just heading there now."

Her head bobs once before she turns on her heel, heading towards the group of tutors lingering on the couch.

Knowing that I sacrificed time to meander by making my coffee, my steps are brisk as I race across campus. Coffee balancing in one hand, I juggle my texts and notebooks in the other.

I'm right on time when I walk into the class and pay no attention to the students already seated. Behind the podium, I pull my drive up on the screen, opening today's presentation before sharing the screen to the massive projector screen behind me. I run through the motions like a robot, following the steps I planned and practiced when I first took the position.

"On Writing" my first slide reads. Because you can't write a creative non-fiction masterpiece if you can't write a good story. Eyes down, focused on my notes before I start my very first lecture, I can't escape the tiny gasp I hear from the front row.

Looking up, I see the worst thing imaginable.

Madison. In my class.

My thoughts scramble and I drop the papers to the floor. Murmurs erupt behind her, no doubt laughing at my clumsiness. They have no idea.

Madison herself isn't the worst thing, she's the best thing I've ever seen. Her blonde hair is pulled back into a tight, low ponytail. Sleek and straight, it's nothing like the messy bundle it became in my fist. The sleeves of her dark green jumper are pulled up, revealing a hint of the floral tattoo on her forearm, and her denim skirt sits tight across her knees.

I want to run my hands along her thighs, pushing that skirt up until I can see if she is wearing those per-fect black panties again.

But shit, I can't.

I can't even think like that anymore, let alone act on my desires.

Madison is in my class. And *that* is the worst thing

possible. Because I have to somehow compose myself and give this lecture to a room full of students.

"Is he okay?"

The voice hesitates, filled with concern, but it blows sense into my lungs all the same. I drop down to pick up the paperwork now strewn about my feet. Hidden behind the podium, I attempt to compose myself. A few deep breaths, a light tap on the sternum. Neither works. But the murmurs grow louder.

Paperwork in my hands, I glance up at the slide and push myself to stand. My notes are completely out of order, but I know this text like I know my own soul. I can do this.

I avoid Madison's gaze when I turn back to the class. Avoid thinking about the nights we shared a bed, or the delicious taste of her.

"On Writing …" I begin, and the rest of the lecture passes in a blur of stumbled words and disinterested students. All of them except Madison. Focusing on the lecture is impossible under her adoring stare.

No matter how hard I try not to look at her, it's like trying not to look at the sun. Her light hauls my eyes toward her. She watches me teach, intently and with adoration. She smiles at my puns, looks concerned when I speak of how hard being an author can be, takes notes when I remind the class of an important point. And it fucking kills me that she is so perfect.

The perfect student. The perfect woman.

One glorious week was all we had, but that was all it took for me to fall. Hard. Fast. Desperately.

"Before your tutorials, try to get some of the reading done," I say to the class as I turn off the projector. "Your tutors will have details of your first assignment."

Chairs empty and a wave of bodies race for the back door. My hands fall to the podium and my head sinks between my shoulders. What a mess.

"Well," her voice cuts through the noise of the students, "that was awkward."

My shoulders shake as I hold in a desperate laugh that wants to escape. Awkward could possibly be the understatement of my entire career.

I can't look at her. If I do, I might kiss her. I might never let go.

"Look at me," she whispers as she steps closer. The podium stands between us, but she leans over it. Her face is so close to mine I can feel the warmth of her breath on my lips. Opening my eyes, I stare into hers. The air in the lecture hall thins until my lungs hurt, unable to suck in the oxygen I need.

Her breasts rise and fall in time with my own heavy breaths, and her eyelids grow heavy. Goosebumps scatter down her arms and a blush rises from her neck. The twisting in my core is back and I feel blood rushing lower.

"I had a really, really, great week."

Madison's fingers trickle along my forearm to toy with the folded sleeves of my shirt. My other arm reaches across the podium. Cupping her cheek, I trail my thumb along her lower lip. Her tongue darts out, following its path.

Logic and reason leave my body. I step around the podium, and she melts into my arms. My arms around her back, I pull our bodies closer and gaze down at her. Whatever she can give me will never be enough.

The side door slams. Jolting apart, Madison scurries to grab her bag from where she left it on the seat.

"Professor Fraser." The high-pitched voice carries around the seating area, giving me pause to gather my thoughts. "How was your first class?"

Her heels click as she patters her way into the room, stopping abruptly when she sees Madison.

"Oh, a student." Professor Dausset's tone sharpens.

"Hi! I'm Madison."

The difference in their voices is stark. Madison's is light and airy, like a summer breeze that leaves a tickle down your spine. Professor Dausset's is filled with bitter disgust. Her hatred for the generation below her sitting deep in her throat.

Her wrinkled eyes dart from me to Madison, then back again. The firm line between her brows deepens. Settling her stare on me, she steps to place herself in front of Madison.

"Interesting." With her pointer finger, she pushes her thin framed glasses up her nose.

"I was just asking Professor Fraser about his decision to add *On Writing* to the reading list at the last minute."

Dausset turns to Madison, arms folded across her chest. "Is it really your business why a professor feels a certain," her arms flail as she finds the word she needs, "text should be read by his students?"

Madison retreats, shrinking into herself as she shakes her head.

"I will remind both of you," Dausset adds, turning back to me, "that while fraternisation between staff and students is generally frowned upon, between a professor and a student it is strictly prohibited."

Madison's mouth drops open. Holding back a cough, I tilt my head to the side.

"I'm well aware." I hold Dausset's gaze, determined not to let her win the staring contest we have somehow entered.

She raises an eyebrow before she turns on her heel, clicking her way back towards the exit.

"I want to discuss your lesson plan," she calls before she opens the door. "Come see me in my office."

As she leaves, the air in the room cools. I blow out a sigh, leaning back against the podium.

That was close. Too close.

"I guess that's why we only had a week." Madison muses.

I nod. Words feel impossible right now. Because I know we only had a week, and I know we have to stick to the rules that have been laid out for us. But one week with Madison will never be enough.

Chapter Five

MADISON

Standing in the hall, I can hear the chatter from inside the faculty break room. Every inch of my body screams at me to turn and walk away. My feet bury themselves against the hard linoleum floor, my knees locked.

I don't want to meet with teaching staff, and I especially don't want to mingle with my fellow scholarship students. There is nothing worse than social events like these.

No. There is nothing worse than sitting in the front row of your first lecture for the year, only to discover that your professor is the insanely attractive man you had been fucking for the past week. That was definitely the worst.

But this faculty meet and greet is an easy second.

I cringe when footsteps make their way down the hall behind me. Not wanting to get stuck one on one with an overachieving creative type, I force myself to move.

Inside the tea room, the noise is overbearing. A hundred conversations float through the air and my brain muddles as it tries to focus on them all. I avoid taking pause to search the people around me. I don't want to know if he is here.

He most likely is. I just don't want to see him.

It was hard enough seeing Oliver this morning. Seeing Professor Fraser this morning.

We never discussed the possibility that I would be in his class. The signs were there. The copy of *On Writing* on his bedside table. The way his gaze lingered on the pile of textbooks on my desk. The fact he is an acclaimed non-fiction writer. But we chose to ignore them all.

I'm glad we did though. We might not have enjoyed ourselves as much if we knew the true size of the hole we were digging.

It certainly would have been nice to have a heads up before this morning though. Creative Non-Fiction was the unit I was most looking forward to in this course. The one that has potential to improve my writing and give me a chance at writing a best-selling book. I want to write what I love, a true blend between romance and travel writing. Fictional stories of people falling in love in real places. But with rejection after rejection, I need to work on the real places part of my writing skills.

Now, I dread the thought of sitting through another lecture. Not because of Oliver. Professor Fraser. But because of us. Because of what we shared. Because of how much more we could have been if the circumstances were only a little different.

The way I feel about him after only a week is stupid. I know that, but I feel it anyway. Sure, we connected on an incredibly physical level. But it was more than that. It was deeper. Like our souls were talking to one another all along.

I should have cut it off as soon as I felt myself falling, but I couldn't. And so, I hit the bottom of the hole and then somehow fell even further. And I have no ladder to help me out of this mess.

A pit forms in my stomach, feeling somewhere between hunger and anxiety. I make my way to the refreshments, wishing I could down a shot to ease my nerves.

Soft drinks line one half of the table, the other loaded with various chips, dip and, oddly, what looks like cut up wedding cake. Pouring myself a drink, I wonder how long I need to stay. I suppose I need make my presence known to at least one faculty member before I leave.

"Hey."

The deep, rusty voice is right by my ear, and I turn to find a young man standing far too close to me. I try to move back, but the table blocks my escape.

The man gestures to my drink with a smirk. "I have something you can add to that."

"No, thank you." I smile, not wanting to cause a scene as I edge my way around him.

My eyes are down as I move away through the crowd. I can't be here anymore. The room is too crowded, too noisy. Too full of people who want to get to know me, and who I have no interest in getting to know right now. Screw finding a faculty member. I need to leave. My ears ring as I rush to the exit.

Reaching for the handle, a firm hand grasps my wrist. His touch spreads warmth up my arm, calming my racing pulse. His woody scent dazes me.

"Are you okay?" Oliver's voice is soft, but even with the incessant noise around us, I hear it perfectly.

I nod. "I just need air."

He doesn't let go of my wrist as he guides me out. Walking down the hallway, he slips his hand down to mine. Our fingers intertwine as we wander. I don't know where we are going, but Oliver does. He tugs me around corners, through doors, and eventually out of the building.

In the dim light, I can make out the basic shapes of the terrace. A tree in the far corner, a bench off to the side and an odd-shaped garden bed in the middle.

Lit only by the light shining through the window on the door, shadows hide most of its beauty.

"What is this place?"

Instead of answering, Oliver pulls me into a firm kiss. I collapse into his arms, allowing him to pull my body towards his.

His lips feel rough on mine, but when he drags his tongue along my lower lip, I open my mouth. Tilting our heads, we deepen the kiss. I savour his taste as our tongues dance together and I feel alive. My heart starts racing again, but not in the jittery, haphazard manner it was before. Now it's sprinting.

Our foreheads rest together when we come up for air. His deep brown eyes see through mine, into my soul, and I want him to see it all.

My hands trail up his chest, toying at the buttons on his shirt. I reach around his shoulders, massaging the nape of his neck, tickling my fingers with the feeling of his buzzed hair.

"What are we going to do?" His voice drops and I catch the hint of sorrow.

Closing my eyes, I consider our options.

Today has made it very clear that we can't stay away from each other. Neither one of us can stand being in the same room as the other without aching to reach out. But if we do, he'll lose his job. I might lose my scholarship. Professor Dausset made that very clear when she nearly caught us earlier today. Strictly prohibited, those were the words she used.

"We hide," I whisper. "We don't get caught."

I hold my breath, waiting for his answer.

Before he can, laughter erupts from the hallway. He pushes me back as the door opens.

Two girls stand, silhouetted in the doorway.

"Oh, sorry!" One of the girls calls out as she drags the other back inside.

"Sorry," the other repeats with a laugh. She turns to her friend asking, "Where do we go now?"

The door starts to close behind them, and I release the air that had caught in my lungs.

"Do you think they saw?"

Oliver shakes his head. "It's too dark out here, they couldn't have seen who we are."

Relief washes over me, and I shake my arms to release the tension.

"But it was close," he adds. "Too close. We can't do this Madison. No matter how much we might want to."

I nod. My throat constricts my eyes start to sting.

Walking away, I get lost in the hall, but I refuse to turn back to him.

We had a week. And we knew it would only be that. I was foolish for even considering we could have more.

Chapter Six

OLIVER

There's a sharp stabbing in my temple as I pull into the car park. The headache has been brewing since last night, and I can't seem to shake it off, no matter how much water I chug.

It probably doesn't help that I haven't slept all week. Instead, I spend my nights tossing and turning. Every time I close my eyes, I see her face. Every time I drift into something that resembles sleep, I dream of her legs wrapped around me. Madison haunts me.

Somewhere around three o'clock this morning I gave up trying. When I couldn't focus on reading, I turned on my laptop. The bright blue light shone through my eyes as I scoured the internet for local charities. I never imagined it would be this hard to donate all my winnings, but I can't find the right place.

Research centres are too focused. Pushing all their efforts into one single type of cancer or a terrible, but singular, disease. Charities raise money for specific groups of disadvantaged minorities, as though no one else has it tough. I want my money to go to everyone. Without discrimination.

At this stage, I'm ready to start throwing cash off the university roof.

I did find one thing in my search last night though, which is why I'm here. At the local community centre. A safe haven for all members of the community. The website boasted nursing services, community classes, food drives, career counselling, financial aid, library services, and a whole host of other outreach programs.

Something for everyone. Which means maybe, I've found my place.

The building has been left in the past, decades older than the new town homes surrounding it. Two potted lemon trees stand tall either side of the ramp that leads the way from the car park up to the bright teal door. Around the side of the building, a small playground is fenced off, and a veggie garden surrounds the car park.

It's homely, nurturing and welcoming in a way that I wasn't expecting.

A soft bell tinkles above the doorway as I enter, and a young man in an orange suit stands up from behind the desk.

"You must be Oliver." His dark eyes meet mine and he smiles.

"I want to reiterate the importance of keeping this confidential."

I shake his outstretched hand. He nods his agreement and gestures for me to enter a small office space. The walls are crowded with filing cabinets, but the window looks out over the playground.

"You mentioned wanting to make a donation?"

"Ten million dollars."

The man freezes, his wide eyes blinking rapidly. Both hands find his chest and his mouth opens to speak. Flustered, he snaps his mouth shut and stumbles over to the chair by the desk.

"I don't even know what we would do with that sort of money." His voice is barely a whisper. Unsure if he was talking to me, or to himself, I choose not to respond.

My attention drifts to the window. Children squeal in delight as they fly down the rickety slide. From this angle, I can see how splintered the wooden structure is. The old plastic pieces might have once been red, but are now a faded, dirty shade of salmon. Sun bears down on the children, whose hats have been strewn about the bark chip that covers the ground.

"You could start by upgrading the playground?"

Mateo leaps out of the chair, as though he forgot I was in the room.

"Yes! Let me show you the centre."

He hops from foot to foot until I nod, then grabs my arm to pull me back into the main room.

We wander through the centre, Mateo pointing out old light fixtures and broken furniture. Down the hall-way, Mateo greets the local Mothers Group, and we poke our heads in on a study session for mature students. He points out the community calendar, outlining all the classes and events happening through the month. The community centre is a place for people from all backgrounds, and warmth spreads through me.

In the far back room, a floristry class is being held.

Mateo drags me in to show me the kitchenette facilities the room offers. The laminate on the bench is peeling, and the tap sits at a precarious angle. Cupboards filled with mismatched crockery and glassware are missing doors.

Spinning to take in the rest of the room, I see her hair before I see her face. But I know it's her. I know those golden strands with the gentle waves. I know the way they tangle in my fist, and how they look spread out on a pillow.

Madison double takes when she sees me. Like a child who can't believe they are seeing their teacher outside of school. The thought is a firm punch to the temple, causing my headache to throb and a pit of nausea to bubble in my gut.

"Oli!"

Coming from anyone else's mouth, I hate that nickname. But from Madison, it's birdsong. I smile back at her as she places her bare stemmed flowers on the table in front of her. She holds up ten fingers, mouthing something that resembles 'wait for me'. As though I had the power to walk away from her.

"I'll speak with my financial planner about a cheque." I tell Mateo once we are back in the closet sized room he calls his office.

He rattles my hand between his, bouncing on his toes as he shakes it up and down.

"We cannot thank you enough."

"Confidentiality, remember." I remind him. The last

thing I need is for anybody to find out I gave away that much money.

A coffee van is parked outside, surrounded by the women from the Mothers Group. I join the queue, hands in my pockets as I wait. For coffee. For Madison.

She finds me sitting on the edge of one of the raised garden beds. My back is to the sun, but it's heat spreads down my neck and under my dark t-shirt.

"Flowers?" She holds them out to me.

I never imagined it would feel this nice to be on the receiving end of a floral bouquet, no wonder women like it. Most of the flowers are white, but scattered between the puffy petals are some small yellow daisies.

"Thank you."

Madison turns to rest next to me. Our thighs touch, tingles spread from the contact, making me shiver.

"So," she starts as she nudges me, "why were you spending your Saturday morning on a tour of the community centre?"

I choke on my sip of coffee. I don't know what to tell her. We started this with a lie that only served to get us into deep water, telling another lie doesn't feel worth it.

"I have some money to donate. Why were you here?"

She grabs the flowers from my hand, whacking me on the head with them before returning them to my lap.

"Floristry class, dummy."

"I thought your sister was the florist?"

"She is. We started coming to this class together. It

was a way to know each other better. I did a florist class with her, she did a writing class with me."

Her shoulders droop. Twiddling her thumbs and shuffling her feet, she hesitates before continuing.

"At least we did."

Forgetting we aren't meant to be together I wrap my arm around her and pull her close. She leans against me in a way that feels natural.

"Turns out I really enjoy playing with flowers. It makes me feel close to her even though she's a plane away."

"It's normal to miss someone."

She sighs into my shoulder.

"Is it normal to miss you?"

My heart acknowledges her admission first, but it spreads through my entire body like wildfire.

"I miss you too."

The sound of cars coming and going from the car park fills the silence between us. We fall into one another, neither ready to move.

"So." Tilting her head up, Madison's mouth is so close to mine it hurts. My lips tingle, begging me to lean down and kiss her. To show her how far I've fallen. "Why are you donating money to the community centre?"

I don't know why, but I tell her everything. About winning the money, about not wanting it, not deserving it. I tell her about the charities I'd researched and how none felt *right*. And I tell her how Mateo and the community centre needs the money, and how they deserve it more than I do.

"They help *everyone*, with whatever they need. Young adults learning to be parents, older adults struggling with technology, kids who need help with their schoolwork. There are no criteria, no boxes to tick before you can get help. They just help."

My gaze drifts away from her to the faded brick building, and maybe it's just the sun but the warm glow spreads through me again.

"Maybe it's stupid to give away ten million dollars. But this feels right."

To her credit, she doesn't baulk or skip a beat when I admit how much money I'm donating.

"I think that's beautiful. I love that you want to help."

Leaning down, I give in to temptation. My lips find her mouth, brushing against her soft lips. I feel her body relax into mine. The kiss is tender and gentle, less ferocious than the ones we shared before. When we part, her cheeks are flushed and her eyes look moist.

"Will I ever not miss you?"

I brush away her tear with my thumb. I miss her too, and I doubt I'll ever stop.

Chapter Seven

MADISON

Walking into my second week of university I have a spring in my step. Seeing Oliver over the weekend threw out every notion I had to forget about him, to pretend our week of bliss never happened. But at the community centre he seemed different. Natural. Calm. Content.

He seemed like himself again.

How he was before I officially became a student and our relationship crossed boundaries. Happiness spread through him in that week. And I saw a hint of that come back as we sat by the garden.

He isn't like that here. Inside these walls he feels closed off. His shoulders are stiff and he never smiles. His laugh is forced. Even his nods are different, short and sharp instead of the enthusiastic head bob I've seen.

I want to know why. Is he putting on a show for someone? Or trying to fit into the mould of how he thinks a professor should act?

Whatever it is, I'm going to get to the bottom of it. I just need to convince him that what we have is worth a little running around. We deserve more than stolen moments behind closed doors, but I will take what I can get.

I shouldn't feel this deeply for a man I've only

known a couple of weeks, but my heart is constantly beating for Oliver. For Professor Fraser. It sounds so wrong, but it feels so right. One week was not enough, and I know there is no turning back for me.

An email notification pings on my phone, earning me a sour look from the student sitting across from me in the library.

"Sorry," I whisper. Pulling my phone out of my bag I switch it to silent before opening the email.

I am irrevocably fucked. The universe is out to get me, and I have no idea what I did wrong to deserve this.

Skimming through the details of my scholarship, I struggle to pay attention to what I'm reading. I can't pull my eyes away from the name of the professor that has been assigned as my advisor.

> From: Creative Arts Director Professor Dausset
>
> Subject: Creative Writing Advisor - Professor Oliver Fraser
>
> Message: A meeting has been scheduled for Tuesday 9.30 a.m. in Professor Fraser's office, located in the CAF building.

Kind of them, to send me an email before the scheduled meeting. Shame it only came through with five minutes to spare. And I don't even know where the CAF building is.

"Shit!"

I scurry to gather my books into my tote while I ask the grumpy student for directions.

"Creative Arts Faculty?" He scoffs.

Of course! Except that it's on the other side of campus. I doubt I'll make it in time, but I rush through the courtyard anyway.

Slamming through the door at 9.34, my chest heaves as I try to catch my breath. Dropping my hands to my knees I attempt to slow pulse.

"Madison?"

Oh God, his voice. It's like every time we are apart, I forget just how deep and guttural his voice is. It tugs at my insides and sends tingles down my thighs. Just as my heart was returning to a stable rhythm, it skips a whole stack of beats before racing away again. Back to the sprint it tends to perform whenever Oliver is around.

I close my eyes, composing myself before I look up.

I should have kept my eyes closed.

He is dressed more professionally than I've seen him. Dark grey suit pants hug his hips, and his shirt is tight over his biceps. With sleeves rolled up, I can see the strength of his forearms. The veins that strain away from the muscle.

My body acts all on its own. I step toward him, reaching for his tie. I tug it, pulling his face towards mine.

"Wait."

I jump back at his hesitation. Crossing my arms around my stomach, I squeeze my hands into my sides to hold them steady.

"Sorry, I shouldn't have—"

Oliver steps past me to close the door. The click

of a lock registers in my brain, and then the heat of his body behind me.

I spin to face him, but his hands hold my shoulders still.

"You are here to discuss your studies," he whispers. The warmth of his words brushes over my pulse point, and I feel it in my core.

"Yes, professor."

A groan escapes him, and his forehead drops to rest on the back of my head.

"Call me that later." Pushing his body into mine, I can feel his erection against my back.

I hadn't meant for my words to do that, but I can't help myself from enjoying his reaction. Leaning back against him, I tilt my head to rest on his shoulder and stare up at him. My tongue darts out to lick my lip.

Oliver groans again but guides me off him and walks towards the desk.

"You have a scholarship, Madison. And I'm your advisor. Whatever else happens between us, that relationship *has* to stay professional. When we have these monthly meetings, your coursework comes first. Everything else comes after."

He brushes a hand through his dark hair as he leans back in the chair.

We spend the next twenty minutes doing exactly what he asked. Discussing my coursework. He makes note of when my assignments are due, checks I have an appropriate study plan in place, and offers his advice on additional texts and references I should be using. Focusing on the paperwork is frustrating, but when he finally closes his laptop to look up at me my fingers tingle in anticipation.

"You seem to have a solid grasp on your coursework, let me know if you need any assistance with anything. You have my number."

I take my time packing my notebooks and planner back into my tote, sliding them in one by one. When Oliver doesn't say anything else, my shoulders droop and a hole opens in my chest. The realisation that I read too much into our situation starts to sting my eyes. I stare up at the ceiling, blinking away the tears that threaten to fall.

"About earlier," my voice cracks, "I'm sorry. I won't do it again."

Hands slam on the desk between us. Professor Fraser stands. He towers over me, and I shift my eyes to look at his face. His eyes are dark, pupils so large I can hardly see the rich brown of his irises. The fire reignites. And I know there is no extinguishing it.

"Nothing like that can ever happen on campus."

I nod, biting my lip but holding his gaze.

"But you will call me professor again." He pushes away from the desk.

I stand from the chair to take a step to unlock the door, pausing before I open it.

"When?"

"Not now."

He stares at the tree outside his window. An arm

stretches up to the window frame. His cock strains his pants, and he uses his other hand to adjust himself.

"Madison," he pleas, "you need to leave before I decide to scrap my own rule and fuck you right over this desk."

My mouth drops open. I squeeze my legs together in a failed attempt to relieve some of the tension that sparks. The last thing I want to do is leave after a comment like that. I drop my bag where I stand by the door and take two measured steps towards the desk.

Oliver growls, turning back into the room.

A knock sounds at the door, and we both jump at the sudden interruption.

"Professor Fraser?" I recognise the voice, the grouchy kid from the library.

Oliver clears his throat before responding for the student to enter. When the door opens, I take my cue to leave, reminded again why campus is out of bounds for Oliver and me.

Chapter Eight

MADISON

Weeks pass in a blur. Wednesdays are the hardest. Sitting, listening to his lecture. Trying not to imagine climbing over the chairs to fall into his arms behind the podium. Trying not to think about the look on his face when I drop to my knees in front of him.

Oliver and I haven't spoken since we found out he was my advisor. Despite the way both of us long for something more, neither of us has reached out to do something about it. Every time I start to type a message, fear freezes my fingers. If he wanted to see me like that, he'd reach out to me. But why would he?

Compared to him … who am I?

He's a professional. Published in at least seven languages, his books are on every bookstore shelf. They're in every library and I've even seen one in an airport. He has had the kind of success I could only dream about, and to top it all off he completed a doctorate to become a professor.

I doubt a man like that would fall for a woman like me. A wannabe with nothing but a casual retail job and a stack of stories that never make it past the first draft. I was just a fling to him. A fling he still finds unbearably attractive, maybe, but just a fling.

It hurts, forcing myself to think this way. But it's better than the hope I feel every Wednesday when I walk into his lecture. When I see the way his eyes linger on me, soaking in every inch of skin while he addresses the class. I bite the inside of my cheek and hold back the goofy smile that fights to escape.

It feels good to be looked at by him. But I hate the way he does nothing about it. My skin crawls as each lecture drags. A million fire ants marching all over me, biting down when the lecture ends and he packs his things, leaving without a hint of a goodbye. It makes me wonder what changed. Did he meet someone else? Someone in his league, or at the very least someone less forbidden. Or did the grumpy library boy suspect something and make a comment? Or worse, did he make a complaint?

Not knowing what happened is a world of confusion and hurt. And I hate myself for finally opening my heart up to someone when I knew it was doomed from the start.

A cool breeze leaves goosebumps on my legs as I walk to the pizza store near my apartment. My new boots rub against my ankles. I push through the pain of oncoming blisters, wishing I wore thicker socks. It's too late now, but the pain will remind me to change them when I get home.

If I decide to go out, that is. According to the flyer, the Student Union Mixer is the biggest event of the semester. I don't care much for mingling, but the open bar for just twenty dollars entry sounds appealing. After the past few weeks spent wallowing, a night out could be just what I need.

Some of the people I've met in my classes will be there, and I know I should make an effort to make friends. With my sister gone, and Oliver AWOL, I have no one to turn to. So, I guess I'll be going to the mixer after all. As soon as I eat a family sized pizza to myself and change my socks.

The pizzeria is packed when I walk in. Every table is surrounded by customers, and the extra benches are overflowing as dozens of people wait for their food. I order my pizza and join the crowd, squeezing myself onto a bench as soon as there is room.

"… barbeque chicken …"

No matter how much I'm trying to ignore the noise inside the pizzeria, I can't help but pinpoint his voice. He is facing the counter, but there is no denying that's Oliver. I should have known he'd be here. After all, it was his favourite pizza shop before it was mine.

I pull my overgrown bangs over my face and stare down at my lap, trying not to be noticed. But when white sneakers step into my line of sight I know I've been spotted.

My eyes trail their way up his body. Grey sweats. Of course, he has to be wearing grey sweats. And of course, I have to be sitting while he stands over me. The bulge in his pants is inches from my face.

I pull my lips into my mouth as I remember how he tasted. How he felt buried deep inside me. My cheeks burn at the memory.

In the sliver of space I occupy, I attempt to search the room. I'm cautious of wandering eyes, but mostly checking there is no one from the university around.

"No one will be here, it's too far from campus."

Oliver reaches out to tuck my bangs behind my ears. His thumb lingers on my cheek, brushing over my lips.

The woman sitting next to me stands. Whether it's because she can sense the friction between Oliver and I, or because her order was called, I don't know. She leaves a tiny spot on the bench, too small for Oliver to sit down, so I move across, away from the old man on my right.

Oliver has other plans. He picks me up, turns me around, then sits down in my spot. Pulling me onto his lap, I wiggle as I fix my dress and feel his length stiffen. It presses against my core, the thin fabrics between us feeling like too much and not enough all at once.

"Student Union Mixer?"

I nod, refusing to turn around, unable to face him. "After I eat."

"Are you meeting someone there?"

"Yes."

He makes a guttural noise against my neck.

"Friends," I clarify, "from class."

His hand stretches over my stomach, holding me in his lap. "Would they miss you?"

They wouldn't, I know they wouldn't. But I don't

know what's going on here. After weeks of not talking to me, now this. I can't help but wonder what took him so long. Why he waited for a chance meeting to make a move.

I squeeze my hands into fists, painting on an armour of confidence I don't feel, and turn to face him. His gentle smile distracts me from my exasperation, but eventually I convince my nose to scrunch and my brow to furrow.

"You haven't spoken to me in weeks."

"I can explain."

The shop bell dings, interrupting us, and the server calls out both our numbers.

I wince when I stand up, the blisters in my boots breaking open at the movement. Oliver grabs hold of my arm, holding me up when I stumble.

"Blisters," I explain.

I hobble to pick up my pizza. Oliver stays close, collecting his own then following me out the door. He heads left, but when I start down the footpath to the right, he pauses.

"You can't walk with blisters."

"I have to."

He shakes his head, walking over to me and handing me his pizza.

"I'll carry you."

I start to protest, but he scoops me up, one arm nestled under my legs and the other supporting my back. Cradled against him, I hold on to the pizzas and decide not to fight this. There's a cool breeze in the night air, but I don't feel it as Oliver carries me home.

He holds me steady while I fetch my key from my bag. He carries me along the ground floor corridor. He holds me tight as he steps across the threshold and into my apartment.

After closing the door behind us, he places me down on the stool by the door. Dropping to his knees, he unzips my boots, sliding them off my feet with care.

"First aid kit?"

I shake my head, pulling him up as I stand.

"I'm okay, I just needed the boots off. Thank you."

We sit on my couch and eat. It feels so natural that I almost forget I was supposed to be mad at him.

"Are you going to explain why you haven't spoken to me?" I remember to ask as I grab the last piece of my pizza.

He leans back on the couch, arms stretching over his head.

"Dausset," he says. "She was suspicious after she saw you in the lecture hall after my class. When she found out I was your advisor she started asking questions."

"I thought she assigned the advisors?"

"Her assistant does it. I'm surprised she even bothered to check the list."

It doesn't take away the pain I felt when he all but ghosted me, but I can at least understand his reasoning. He could lose his job if the university ever finds out about us. More than that, he could lose his entire career. His credibility. His book deals. Everything.

"I get it." I rest my head on the arm he has draped behind me.

"There is nothing I want more than this, but you deserve more." He sits up, pulling me with him and turning our bodies on the couch until we are face to face. "I can't take you out to dinner or hold your hand on campus. Everything we do has to be in private. You deserve to be with someone you don't have to sneak around with."

"I don't need those things. I don't need a public relationship. I just need to know you're there for me." I lean closer to him. So close our lips are nearly touching. "I just need you."

Chapter Nine

OLIVER

I shouldn't be here. Neither should Madison. She should be out, at the student party, celebrating the first few weeks of semester with her friends.

"I just need you." She whispers the words right into my mouth, and they take every decent thought I have with them. Blood charges through me, my hands tensing against the couch either side of Madison's thighs.

I want her so bad I can't breathe. I need her more than I need the oxygen in this room. The memory of the rhythm our bodies made when we were together surges through me, urging me to close the tiny gap between us.

"Please." Her voice shakes.

Fuck it.

I close the gap, claiming her mouth and pulling her onto my lap. Our bodies press together, chests rising in sync. The longer we kiss, the more frenzied we become. Tongues tangling, we get lost together. My hands are firm on Madison's waist, holding her close.

We fall into place, Madison tilting her head to the side to deepen the kiss. When she grinds her hips, I groan into her mouth.

Everything she gives me will never be enough, but I plan on taking it anyway.

Hands under her waist, I stand and she wraps her legs around me. Walking to the bedroom, I pause by the mirror in her hallway. Her skirt has bunched around hips, and I have a delicious view of her ass in my hands. Round globes, scarcely contained by the red lacy panties. I nip at the delicate skin below her ear, grabbing firmly where my hands meet her flesh. My fingers stretch to pull at her panties. Tugging them to the side with one hand, I trail a finger through her soaking folds.

She makes a whimpering sound in my ear that pulses through my cock. I thrust my fingers into her, causing her to moan. With the memory of how she feels wrapped around me, I pull out my fingers and race the last few steps into the bedroom. Dropping her on the bed with force, I reach for the buttons on her dress.

Madison sits herself on the edge of the bed, pulling at the elastic band on my sweats. Her eyes stay on mine as she tugs at the tie and lowers my pants. My cock bounces free, so fucking close to her perfect mouth. Wrapping her hands around my length, she pumps hard. A glistening bead forms at the tip, until she swipes it with her thumb.

She brings her hand to her mouth, licking me off her fingertip. Her lips turn up, a cheeky twinkle in her eyes as she spreads her legs. I step forward, finding my place between them as I unbutton her dress. I massage the mounds of her breasts, pulling her bra down to pinch at her nipples. The sensitive buds are already firm, and she arches her back, forcing her breasts deeper into my hands.

Everything about this moment is perfect. I can feel the warm air from her mouth on my cock. The sensation sends lightning down my spine. I reach down to cup her cheek, tilting her head up to look at me.

"Show me what a good little student you are."

Her tongue wets her lips, and I can feel the warmth spread through her body. I can see the pool of wetness forming in her panties.

"Yes, professor."

Her eyes are still locked on mine as she opens her mouth and drags her tongue from the base of my cock, right up to the tip. She smiles as she tastes the pre-cum that's leaking out.

With one hand on my balls, the other guides my cock into her gorgeous, open mouth. I groan at the tight wetness of her lips. My hips unintentionally thrust at the feeling. Madison swallows me deep, her mouth hollowing out as she takes me back into the depths of her throat. I try to pull back, but she holds me there, humming as she relaxes around my firm length.

"Good … fucking … girl."

The words are strained as I fight the urge to pull at her hair and take control. Her moans vibrate along my shaft, sending a fire through my veins. She bobs her head, massaging my balls. The pressure builds to an intensity I can't keep up with. I need to slow down because I want more than just her mouth. I want everything.

Pulling away, I lift her legs to rest them over my arms. She falls back on the bed and her blue eyes meet mine, I see through the moment into the soul of the woman I love. And I realise that there is no escaping this for me.

Reaching for the bedside table, I pull a condom from the drawer. I tear the foil wrapper with my teeth before hastily rolling the condom down my aching length.

My fingers coast along the seam of her panties, now drenched with her need. Yanking the red fabric to the side, I tear them off her. The slight gasp that escapes her surges me forward. I drive into her in one swift movement, before pausing. Buried deep inside her is the best place imaginable, and I never want to leave.

"Move, please." She pants, bucking her hips. "Professor."

The word has me thrusting, consumed by the forbidden nature of our relationship. Hooking both of her legs over one shoulder, I reach down to rub her clit with my thumb. Her walls constrict around me, dragging my orgasm along with hers.

"Fuck, Madison." I groan as we come together.

Collapsing onto the bed, Madison snuggles into my shoulder. We lay together as we catch our breath.

"Is this really going to work?"

I breathe deep as I tilt her head up. Mascara has run down her face, and her cheeks are still flushed, and I have never seen anything so beautiful. So perfect. So … mine.

"It has to," I whisper before I kiss her.

Work is going to be a nightmare, I know that. I dread Wednesday morning when I walk into that lecture hall, see her shining from the front row, and can't do anything about how much I love her. I hate the thought of ignoring how we feel about each other when we are in public.

Gears start turning in my head, trying to figure out how we can make this work. How I can be with the woman I love without losing my job.

The thought slams into me as I trail my fingers along Madison's shoulder. The only thing stopping us from being together is my job.

The work I've never enjoyed suddenly feels like even more of a burden. It's my own personal prison, and I'm just about ready to break out.

Chapter Ten

MADISON

For a library, there's a lot of chatter this morning. I can only assume the weekend's party is to blame for the extra conversation. Across from me, two girls gossip about the guys they went home with. Down one aisle, a couple has a not-so-subtle argument about boundaries. And the student librarians are huddled around a book cart laughing.

The teeniest, tiniest part of me wishes I could join in the conversation. I want to tell the girls at the table how I win. Their guys have nothing on mine. But I know that I can't. I know why I can't.

Oliver cooked me breakfast yesterday morning, and we spent the day tangled in the bedsheets. I told him I was okay with sneaking around. Now that I'm doing it, though, it's hard. It hasn't even been twenty-four hours but being in love and not being able to scream it to the world sucks.

Head down, I try to focus on the text in front of me. The words jumble, blurring on the page until it's impossible to focus. It's not until the nausea hits that I realise I'm about to lose my peripheral vision.

I lose my balance as I stand, searching my tote for my migraine medication. Finding a wafer, I peel it open.

The minty flavour causes a rush of relief through my body, but my eyes are still struggling to focus. I'm too late. I need to find somewhere dark. Quick.

The girls on the other end of the table glance up at me, their eyebrows drawn together. One tilts her head, opening her mouth to speak before closing it again. I want to tell them I'm okay, but the words catch in my throat.

Stumbling toward the exit, my hands reach for every surface so I don't fall. I can't see to either side, can't turn my head to make sure I don't walk into anything.

The exit is so close when I see him. Standing at the end of an aisle, pulling a book from the returns trolley. My shoulders relax as I head to him, feeling safe. I know I shouldn't, I know I'm putting everything at risk, but right now I need his help.

"Oli—" I pause when he gives his head a tiny shake. I swallow down the lump in my throat and try again.

"Professor Fraser."

He nods at me, turning back to the book he had pulled from the shelf. I stand next to him, not too close to look suspicious.

"I need you," I whisper.

But he shakes his head, taking a step away from me. His eyes are still on the book when he answers me, so quietly I barely hear him.

"Not here." He glances down the aisle and I look up to see Professor Dausset deep in conversation with another student.

As though she felt my eyes on her tight bun, she glares up at me. Her eyes dart between Oliver and me, a line forming between her brows. With tight lips, she turns her attention back to the student.

Oliver can't help me.

"Sorry." The word is nothing but an exhale as I turn on my heel and scurry out of the library.

The light as I cross the courtyard is far too bright, but I duck through shadows towards the main building. Inside, I find my way to an empty classroom. The screen by the door says it's free for the next three hours. I log myself into the room, muscle memory working to reserve the room for as long as possible.

Sensor lights blind me when I enter, but I'm counting on them turning off when I stop moving. Bundling my jacket around my bag, I curl up on the floor, facing the corner. My hands cover my face until the lights flick off and the medicine starts to ease the thumping in my brain.

I wake up to the sound of my alarm, sticky with sweat. I don't remember setting it, but the clock shows I have half an hour before someone else has booked the room, so I must have been thinking straight even when I wasn't thinking at all. My back aches as I roll to a seated position. My throat is dry and my eyes feel heavy, but my head isn't pounding.

It's been a long time since I've had a migraine that intense. Although that's probably attributed to the fact that I usually spot them sooner. The earlier I can get a wafer on my tongue, the more effective the sickly-sweet medicine is. But I was too distracted earlier, I didn't notice the signs.

My brain still feels foggy, but my stomach drops at the hazy memory of how Oliver had brushed me off.

He hadn't even given me a chance to tell him what was happening. There's a part of me that hopes he would have acted differently if he knew, but an equal sized part wonders if that's true.

The boundaries we had set were to protect him, not me. His job, his reputation, his career, it's all on the line if anyone finds out about us. There's every reason to think that he wouldn't risk any of that just because I was in pain.

I can't rely on Oliver any more than I could rely on my mother, or my sister. I was stupid to think that I could after we established the secrecy of our relationship. Day one and there I was trying to break the rule we set.

My phone pings again and I pull it out of my bag. It was never an alarm. Messages from Oliver flash on the screen.

Oliver: Are you okay?

Oliver: Madison, what happened?

Oliver: It's been hours, I'm sorry I brushed you off, but Dausset was right there.

Oliver: I'm in my office, come see me. Please.

I don't want to go. Not like this. Not when my brain still feels foggy, and I know I need another few hours of sleep—preferably on a bed this time. Not when I don't know how to feel about what happened in the library.

If I go, all I'll want to do is crumble into him and rest in the comfort of his arms. But I can't. Never on campus. That's what he said. That's what we agreed.

I push my hair back from my face, rubbing my eyes with my palms.

Madison: I'm okay.

The reply is blunt, but it's all I feel like giving.

Chapter Eleven

MADISON

The sun is still too bright this morning, despite the overcast grey cloud cover. After sleeping the rest of the day away yesterday, I woke up this morning feeling groggy, and panicked.

My first assignment is due at 5 p.m. today, and so far, all I've done is jot down some references to support my case. The 500-word essay should be easy, and I had planned on spending all day yesterday writing and polishing it. That plan dropped off a cliff, but if I write 100 perfect words an hour, I'll get it done on time.

Inside the library, I pull my dark sunglasses off my face. The world blurs for a moment as I trade them out for the clear frames I usually wear. Finding a seat, I open my laptop and spread the photocopied texts out. I spend too long reading and re-reading the question. Longer still trying to form a solid opening paragraph. I can write a 3000-word creative piece at the drop of a hat; this essay should be a walk in the park.

But it's not.

Trying to convey my own thoughts whilst also backing up every claim I make with an appropriate reference is like trying to fact check the world building of a fantasy novel. Long, arduous, and impossible.

After an hour, I've only written 80 words. Half of those don't count. References, subheadings, my name.

"Fuck." I whisper the words to myself as I drop my head to the desk. Thankful that I chose a table deep in the corner of the library, I close my eyes and give myself ten minutes to refocus.

I allow myself a moment of self-pity. Doubt spreads through me, squeezing at my rib cage. If I hadn't spent the weekend with Oliver, I would have made more progress before the migraine hit yesterday. I might even have finished the essay. Instead, I wasted away my time, getting lost in the feel of his body. Imagining a world where we could be together.

Just months ago, I never would have fallen into such a fantasy, but something about Oliver has me digging this hole myself. And it needs to stop.

My neck aches, my brain is fuzzy, and bricks settles on my shoulders. I know what I need to do, but asking for help is going to hurt. In more ways than one.

Madison: Professor Fraser, I need to discuss something with you. Can we meet this afternoon?

Dancing dots appear as he writes his reply.

Oliver: Madison, are you okay?

Madison: Yes, I just need some assistance.

Oliver: My office? 3.30 p.m.

Madison: See you then.

I'll be cutting it close, but I'm placing all my bets on Oliver being able to help me out of this mess. Professor Fraser is my advisor after all.

Instead of attempting to continue working on my coursework, I find a soft patch of grass in the courtyard. Under the shade of the tree, I lean back against my bag and play an audiobook through my headphones. Of all the things I should be doing, all the texts I should probably be reading for my classes, I'll never give up my love for romance novels. Even if they have made my expectations for love sky high.

Maybe that's why I had fallen for Oliver in the first place. The forbidden nature of the relationship, the way he was willing to risk it all to be with me. Until yesterday, when he showed me that wasn't actually the case. The realisation that he wasn't like the men in the romance novels made the whole thing feel worse than it really was.

I know I can't turn to him on a personal level, but I'm hoping I can count on him on a professional one.

His door is open as I approach his office. Before I enter, I take in the sight of him. Leaning back in his chair, his arms stretch behind his head. The desire to crawl under his desk and taste him again surges through me. Hot lava settles between my legs. Fuck. Why does the man have to look so good in a shirt?

"Professor Fraser."

He looks up from his laptop, the corner of his lip turns up in a smirk.

"Madison, I'm glad to see you." One hand reaches between his legs. Another eruption rushes through me.

I push the door closed, stumbling over my words, fighting for my academic brain to stay in control of the situation.

"I need help," I mumble, avoiding his gaze.

"Come here."

He stands. His hard length tight against the zipper of his pants, drawing my attention to his body. Reaching behind his back, he twists the blinds closed.

"I'm sorry about yesterday. In the library."

"Don't be." I shake my head. "It was my fault. I wasn't thinking straight."

My traitorous body takes a step towards him, my fingers ache to reach forward and stroke his length. But I am not here for sex. I let out a slow, shaky breath, urging the heat inside me to cool.

"I have an assignment." I blurt out the words in one quick gasp. They shock sense into us both. As though a security wall has shot up between us, we step away from each other.

The bridge of Oliver's nose scrunches. Reaching down, he adjusts himself before stepping to sit back down. I take the seat on the other side of the desk, pushing it back so I can't reach him, even if I wanted to.

"Do you need help interpreting the question?"

"No," I shake my head. "It's your question about perspective in non-fiction writing. I need an extension."

A short puff of air escapes his mouth. He leans to one side, running a hand through his hair.

"I can't do that."

"I had a migraine yesterday." I try to make him understand. "That's why I needed you in the library, and it's why I need your help now. Only, I need your academic help. I couldn't see, couldn't think. I took medication that made me sleep all afternoon and my brain still feels as though the aerial isn't connected properly. I can't focus and I only have 80 words written."

His shoulders sink. Dropping his head, he closes his eyes and presses fingers into his temples. He looks back at me with a stony expression, his mouth forming a thin straight line.

"I'm sorry."

Holding my breath, I wait for him to continue.

"I'm sorry about yesterday in the library. If I knew you needed help, I would have acted differently. Dausset is suspicious, but I would have figured something out. But I can't give you an extension."

My eardrums throb. "Why not?"

"There's a formal process. It's too late now."

The air in my lungs turns to lead. If I miss an assignment, I risk losing my scholarship.

"My advice is to submit what you can. I know you've done the reading and am confident you can whip together a passing grade to avoid jeopardising your scholarship."

Leaning forward, he reaches a hand across the desk. I don't take it. Frozen on the spot I force my head to bounce a sharp nod. Acknowledging what he has said is one thing, processing it is another.

"You can stay here while you work."

"No, thank you." I need to get out. I can't stand to be in the same room as him.

Screw university policy. Screw relationship boundaries. I needed him. Twice now. And both times he let me down. Spectacularly.

I have an hour to scramble 450 words together into something that resembles an essay. Storming my way out of his office to head back toward the library, I ignore the way his voice catches as he calls my name.

Never again, I promise myself as I blink away the tears that threaten to escape. This is what happens when I open myself up to counting on someone. And I will never do it again.

Chapter Twelve

OLIVER

Darkness consumes my office. The assignment deadline is approaching, and with it a summer storm rolls across the sky. Dark clouds echo the heaviness in my mind.

I can't sit still as I wait to see Madison's assignment land in my inbox. Tossing a stress ball between my hands, I pace around the tiny office. At each corner, I kick the legs of my solid wood desk. My shoes are scuffed and my toes hurt, but I continue the self-inflicted torture.

With a minute to spare, the gentle ding of a new email sounds through my laptop. Noticing it's not Madison's submission, I throw the stress ball against the wall. It hits my framed doctorate certificate. Glass shatters, the sound only serving to fuel my anger further.

I'm not angry at Madison. How could I be? She did nothing wrong.

I'm angry at myself. For letting her down. For unwittingly showing her that she was right, that she can't rely on anyone other than herself. I hate that my actions reinforced those feelings. When all I want is for them to be as far from the truth as possible. I hate that in her moment of need, I chose to follow the rules. I chose not to stretch them on compassionate grounds, regardless of our history.

When I took this job, I thought I could make a change. I thought I'd be different. But I'm not. I'm just another professor expecting perfection from my students. I'm not teaching them how to think creatively, how to make their passion shine. I'm teaching them to follow the rules, to step in line and stay in their lane. And it's not what I wanted.

Another ding sounds, and I rush to check the screen.

From: Madison Fisher

Subject: Madison Fisher – Assignment 1 – Creative Non-Fiction

Reading the email subject, my heart squeezes. First at her name, and again as it acknowledges that she did it. I don't even care if it's three pages of dribble. She got the assignment in on time. Now I just need to find a way to make it up to her. To show her that I'm sorry.

Snatching my phone from my desk, I pull up her details and hit call.

The phone rings out, and I wonder if it means she doesn't want to talk to me. Maybe I'm showing the age gap between us by calling instead of firing off a text. But short written exchanges have no tone, and I need to get these words right.

Oliver: I'm sorry for earlier. I'm sorry for a lot of things. Can I see you tonight?

My eyes widen at her response.

Madison: Don't be sorry, you have a job to do. But there are some things we need to discuss. I can meet you at your place after dinner.

On the tram ride back to my townhouse, my shoes feel like concrete slabs, weighing me down. Saying sorry is never easy, but I'm dreading Madison's reaction. Her message felt so cold. So clinical and formal. Not at all her usual upbeat self. I shouldn't be surprised, after how I treated her. And I know I'm going to have a lot of grovelling to do.

***

Clearing my uneaten dinner off the plate, the pit in my stomach expands. My heart and lungs fall into its depths. Madison didn't say what time she would be here, and waiting for her arrival feels like walking on a bed of nails.

Her knock at the door forces a sharp inhale. I choke on saliva as I make my way up the hall to let her in.

Standing on the doorstep in jeans and a simple tee, her black cardigan hangs open over her shoulders. I can't help but notice her gentle curves. The way her shirt stretches, just a fraction, over her breasts, how her jeans hug her hips. I want to pull her into me, to sink my teeth into her flesh and mark her as mine. But seeing the look on her face, I hold myself back.

She's been crying. Her eyes are puffy and swollen, and salty marks line her cheeks where her tears have dried. Tiny creases form between her brows, and her lower lip is covered in red marks from her teeth. My throat closes. Knives form in the pit inside my stomach, piercing me from the inside out. I made her feel that way.

"Come here," I whisper, reaching out to guide her inside.

"No."

My hand drops at the sharp tone. My heart stops beating.

"I have to say this here," she continues, "and quickly."

I nod, keeping my mouth shut to give her time to say her piece. But I know what's coming. I read between the lines of her message. I can tell from the look on her face and the way she won't come inside.

"It was only supposed to be a week. We made that deal, and then we both broke it. And I tricked myself into thinking we could somehow make this work, despite all the giant red flags warning me against us. Warning us both. It's not your fault, because I know you have a job to do, but your actions over the past two days showed me why we can't do this. They showed us both why we will never work. I can't rely on you when I need you. You can't jump to my aid whenever something goes wrong. And I need someone who can. I deserve someone who can."

My head pounds. I sway against the door frame as my limbs turn to jelly and I can't breathe. I can't speak.

I can't think. I just feel. My entire body cracks in two for the woman standing in front of me. I feel the way I let her down when she needed me, and I hear her trying to justify it as though it's okay.

"It's my fault." The words fall out of my mouth on a mumble, and I almost expect her to tell me I'm wrong, but she doesn't. Instead, she folds her arms across her chest and nods. It is my fault.

My knees buckle under the weight of dread. I drop my hands to my thighs, barely holding myself up. I'm prepared to beg.

"Get up." She takes a step back. "Get up. Don't beg me for something I can't give you. For the first time in my life, I'm the one walking away. I'm choosing me. You need to let me have this."

"I'm so sorry."

I push myself to stand upright. As soon as my face is level with hers, Madison turns in place, pausing for only a moment before walking away. I watch as she leaves down the street. I watch and I feel my heart fall after her.

Chapter Thirteen

OLIVER

Pulling into the car park of the community centre, I notice that nothing has changed. The veggie patch walls are still pushed to a tilt under the strain of overgrown grass and dirt. The swing still creeks in the playground.

A sliver of disappointment claws its way up my back. Rolling my shoulders, I force it down. Between organising the cheque and the funds clearing through the banks, they've only had the money I've donated for a couple of weeks. Transferring such a large sum is, I've learned, not a simple process.

It would be unfair of me to expect them to have made immediate changes. But as I walk toward the entrance, I notice that they have added at least one thing. A wooden plaque has been fixed above the door.

Fraser Community House

So much for confidentiality. I'm grateful, at least, that the surname is common. Kind of. I hope.

"Oliver!" Mateo greets me with a hug. In navy suit pants and a flamingo pink shirt, he somehow looks more fabulous than the first time we met.

With my arms pinned at my sides, my back stiffens. Mateo bounces in the embrace.

"Mateo." His name is deep in my throat, a greeting, but firm enough to warn him of my discomfort.

"Sorry, it's just been a wonderful few weeks." He leans back in and adds with a whisper, "All thanks to you."

"You asked me to come see you?"

He nods, stepping towards his office. I follow him inside, taking a seat on the small stool on this side of the desk.

"We need a new board member." His voice holds an airy feel. Tone rising, as though he expects a response to a question he still hasn't asked.

"We can't make any decisions regarding the money until we have a complete board. We have plans, projects, proposals. So much is in place, but the chairman is adamant. Even though they have been trying to get someone on board for months, he won't budge. Until they find someone suitable, all the donation can do is look pretty in the bank account."

I consider what he is telling me and wonder why I didn't find out about it sooner. Would it have swayed my decision if I had known the money couldn't be immediately spent? There's a possibility. But I also know that this is exactly the kind of place I wanted the money to go.

"What kind of qualifications does a board member need? Is it a paid position?"

"It pays. No amount to write home about, but enough to get you by." He shrugs. "As for qualifications, they care more about the changes someone wants to make in the community than their degree. Although a doctorate doesn't hurt."

Point made. And his urgent request for a meeting this morning is starting to make more sense.

I can't believe I'm considering this, but the thought of returning to the university makes my shoulders shake. The shudder rushes down my body, depositing cement in my stomach.

This could be the answer to everything. I just don't know if it's too late.

I might have put on a brave face for this meeting, but a dagger rests in my chest. I'm scared that if I try to pull it out, I'll bleed out on the faded carpet. Every time I blink, I see Madison as she walked away. I see the puffiness of her eyes, the way her shoulders sagged under the weight of her heartbreak. And it kills me. With every blink the dagger pushes its way a little further in. Tearing open my heart and crushing my soul.

"Talk to me." Mateo stands from his chair. "I saw you with the young woman. She's a student, isn't she?"

"How could you tell?"

"I have a way." He waves a hand in front of his face. "But that's not important. I saw the way you looked at each other. Like she was the sun, and you were the moon. Two bright bodies in the sky, but you're only alight because of her."

Bingo, that's exactly how I feel. She lights up everything, and everyone around her.

"We met before we knew, but yes. She is a student."

"And that is why I wanted to talk to you about the position. Take some time to think about it. But promise me that you will."

I nod, exiting the tiny office and retreating to my car.

Even if I took this job, if I left the university and we could be together in the way that she deserves, would she still want me? After all the pain I caused, I doubt it. She said she was choosing herself, and I respect that, but I need her to choose me too. To choose us.

I need to know she is on our side before I change everything.

Driving to work, I can't focus. Mateo's words turn over in my head, adding to the battling emotions inside my head. Inside my soul.

I'm still thinking about them as I gather my notes from my office, and I'm still thinking about them when I enter the lecture hall. One look. One look at her and I'll know what to do. I'm sure of it.

But she isn't there. Her front and centre seat is bare, revealing the faded burgundy felt where hundreds of students have sat before. I search the rows, looking for my sun, but she isn't anywhere.

My hands shake as I connect to the screen and straighten my notes. I fumble words, lose my place, forget how to start the slideshow correctly. Someone from far back in the room asks if I'm okay, but I brush them off.

Despite doing my best to finish the lecture, I fall marvellously short. It was a mess. I'm a mess. I knew I hurt her, but for her to not come to class. *Fuck.* I've really messed this up. It's not like her to skip class, to put her scholarship at risk. Even with everything that fell to pieces between us, I never imagined she wouldn't show up to my lecture.

I need to find her. But first I need to make a call.

My phone is out of my pocket before I've finished dismissing the class. It only rings twice.

"Professor Fraser."

Mateo's voice is shrill as he answers the phone.

"Mateo, who do I have to call?"

"Me, you call me."

Air escapes in a grunt.

"Not you. Who do I call about the board position?"

"Me, Oliver. I'm the chairman. You want it?"

This feels too easy, but I'm too worked up to care.

"I want it."

Hanging up the phone, I race to the one place on campus Madison might be. The place I know she loves. The place we both love. The place we met.

Chapter Fourteen

MADISON

I feel like a coward. I guess I am, hiding away in my corner of the library when I'm supposed to be in class. It puts my scholarship at risk, but the alternative was facing Professor Fraser. And I can't bring myself to do that.

Not yet.

Maybe not ever.

I want to forget about the week we spent together, and the short-lived dream that we could make our relationship work. I never want to remember how much it hurt when I realised it wouldn't. Mostly, I want to forget about how he looked when his knees dropped, begging me not to leave.

It took everything I had not to give in. I'm proud of myself for holding my ground and walking away. I deserve to be more than someone's secret. And although it hurts like a bitch now, I'm proud that I stood up for myself.

For the first time in my life, I was the one to walk away. I relied on myself.

I'm just going to hide and cry about it for a few days, that's all.

The words I'm trying to read blur, but it's not the

start of a migraine this time. My eyes well up as I try to read *On Writing*. Knowing it's Oliver's favourite book makes it so much harder to read. I thought using this time to prepare for the next assignment would make me feel better about not being in class. It hasn't.

If anything, it's made me feel worse.

A wet splodge appears on the pages under me, and I give up. Closing the book, I allow the tears to fall.

Crying, alone in the library. It sucks. And I've done it twice now.

What a wonderful start to the year. To my degree.

I want my sister. Pulling out my phone and punching in her number, I hesitate before pressing call. Remembering that she left me to handle university alone is like another boot to the gut. My thumb hits the button before I can overthink calling her.

"Madison!" Her voice is robotic over the phone but comforting all the same.

"Hey."

"Oh God Mads, it's the professor, isn't it?"

I love how she knows me so well. How I never have to tell her what's going on or how I'm feeling. Being so close in age, our almost-twin status drew us closer than any other siblings I know.

"Did he—"

"No Cass, I did." I gasp for air, holding back the sobs forming in my throat. "I walked away because I didn't want to have to hide."

"Oh Mads, I'm sorry."

Her silence comforts me, lets me process a fraction of the aching I feel all over.

"I'm proud of you."

"Me too."

From towards the entrance, the sound of books falling jolts me out of my bubble.

"Cass, I love you. I'll call you later?"

"I love you too."

Hanging up the phone, I cast my gaze over my limited view of the library. Nothing seems out of the ordinary, but librarians hush in vain at whoever caused the commotion. The library is no longer quiet. It hadn't been busy, but there were enough students floating around that quiet, gossip-like chatter starts to spread.

"He is too hot for a professor."

"Normally, sure, but why does he look so frantic?"

"What is he doing?"

The voices from the aisle adjacent to where I'm sitting catch my attention. Surely, they can't be talking about Professor Fraser? He should be teaching. He should be running the class I'm intentionally skipping. He should not be in the library. Looking frantic.

A tiny bead of light sparks in my chest. I refuse to let it grow. Hope is unreliable. Unstable, never constant. Always disappointing. No matter how hard I try, I can't turn off its light.

"Professor Fraser, are you okay?" Her piercing voice cuts through the chatter, putting the hushing of the librarians to shame. Silence spreads through the library.

"Not now."

His voice fuels the spark I was trying to put out. The power surges through me, causing me to stand. He steps around the corner looking like he has been running. His hair is dishevelled and he pants as he skids to a stop.

"Oliver?"

"Madison." My name is a mere whisper on his lips.

"How did you find me?"

He pulls his shoulders to his ears, holding his shrug before letting them drop.

"I had a hunch."

This isn't fair. I wanted to get away from him, not make him come find me. His eyes look bloodshot, a deep maroon instead of their usual chocolate brown. He looks how I feel. Heartbroken and worn down.

"I'm so sorry." He whispers the words as he steps towards me. They melt into the flame in my chest.

"We can't do this here."

Arms folded, Professor Dausset watches us from the aisle. Her eyebrows reach her hairline as Oliver takes another step towards me.

"We can."

My arms drop to my sides as Oliver steps around the table. His hands find my shoulders and he spins me to face him.

"I love you," he says, "and we can."

Time stops.

Our foreheads touch first, a tender, gentle whisper of a touch. Then his mouth finds mine and the tiny spark bursts into fireworks. Oliver gives everything in this kiss, and I feel every piece of longing, of trust, of desperation that he gives me. My arms wrap around him. His hands creep their way into my hair.

Tilting my head, he deepens the kiss, running his tongue along my lips. Opening my mouth, we become more frenzied as we claim each other. As we make our love known. To everyone.

A shrill cough interrupts us. "Professor Fraser!"

Thin, wrinkled hands pull mine off Oliver. They pull me back until the distance between us too great and it hurts all over again. I can see the look in everyone's eyes and the reality of what we just did rings in my ears. Oliver's eyes don't move from mine.

"I'm sorry." I mouth the words but he shakes his head with a smile.

"Professor Fraser." Dausset steps between us, facing Oliver with her hands on her hips. "As you are well aware this type of behaviour is grossly inappropriate. I cannot ignore what you have done here."

"I don't care. I love her."

My mouth drops at his words.

"That is irrelevant. As a professor at this university, you are bound by the moral obligations as laid out in your contract."

"Then I quit."

"Excuse me?" Her already high voice reaches another octave.

What? He quits?

"I quit." He repeats, stepping around his former boss to hold my hand.

"You can't quit because of me." Ignoring all the bystanders, I turn to Oliver. His hand squeezes mine, tugging me towards him.

"I'm not quitting because of you." He steps closer, so our bodies are pressed together. "I'm quitting because of us."

My nose wrinkles, not quite understanding the difference between the two.

"You are the most beautiful person I've ever known. Not just your looks, but your soul. You are inquisitive and generous, and you care about things most people don't. I don't know when it happened, but a little piece of my heart latched onto your soul. But you? I'm not quitting for you. I should be keeping my job for you. So I can keep acting as your advisor and help you become the writer you're destined to be."

He pulls me in, somehow even closer now, until our whole bodies are pressed together. My feet in between his, I can feel the inside of his legs against my own. Our chests rise and fall in sync, and our noses touch.

It feels like home, here in the library surrounded by the books we both love. I don't care about the students and staff members gawking at us. I don't care that our words aren't private. Because I know that he is saying them for me.

"I'm quitting because of us." Oliver clarifies again, planting a firm kiss on my lips. "I'm quitting because despite all of that, I know we are destined to be together. And I can't wait four years for that. I don't want to wait another minute before the world knows that you're mine. That I'm yours. I love you so deeply it hurts to think that we almost never were.

"I should have been the happiest man on the planet, winning all that money. But I wasn't, I was miserable. Until you blasted your way into my life like a shooting star. You lit up my darkest moments and I will do anything, everything, to prove to you that we are more important than a job."

Every admission works to fill the hole in my heart that, moments ago, was only growing larger.

"I'm sorry that it took me so long to realise how important you are. How important we are. It kills me that I hurt you. That I became another person that you thought you couldn't rely on. But I'm here to tell you that you can rely on me. Today, tomorrow, forever."

My heels rise from the floor. Stretching up on my toes, I kiss him.

"It was never your fault," I tell him. "I should never have acted like it was."

I tilt my head, encouraging him to deepen the kiss. His tongue brushes against mine and tingles spread through my entire body. Heat rises from my core and I can feel his length hardening against my stomach.

"I love you." I pull away just enough to whisper into his mouth. "Please, take me home."

Chapter Fifteen

OLIVER

She loves me. The hairs on the back of my neck tickle with goosebumps as she pulls away from the kiss to tell me that she loves me. My heart swells, stops beating, then picks up again at a rapid pace.

With Madison's body pressed up against mine, every sensation feels like too much. Her breasts brush against my chest, her legs settled in between mine. There's no part of me that doesn't have contact with her, but I still ache for more.

"Please, take me home."

She doesn't have to ask twice. I sweep her into my arms, scooping her bag off the table beside us. Her legs wrap around me and she hooks her feet at my lower back. Somehow, I don't collide into anything as we make our way out of the library, never pausing our now desperate kiss. Cheers and whoops surround us as we make our way to my car, and I briefly wonder how quickly the news has spread. It doesn't matter though. All that matters is that Madison is in my arms. She owns my heart. And she is letting me in hers.

Driving home is painful. The buzz from the radio doing nothing to fill the needy silence between us.

Anticipation fills the air and when we finally cross the threshold to my townhouse, there's no holding us back.

Our hands are a frenzied tangle, hers racing to unbutton my shirt while mine tug away at her open cardigan. Reaching into her tank I palm her breast, rubbing the taut bud between my fingers.

"Oli." She moans my name, cutting herself short with a gasp when I pinch my fingers together. I drag her sleeves down her arms. My hand doesn't leave her breast as I lean to take the other in my mouth. My teeth graze against her nipple, and her moans cause an aching in my balls.

Kneeling between her legs, I palm her centre, breathing in her sweet and musky scent. I stretch her leggings and panties down her waist, dropping them on the floor beside me to plant a kiss at the apex of her thighs. Her hands tug at my hair, pulling me closer. I oblige, running my tongue through her seam before flicking at her clit. Her whole body shudders as I push a finger deep into her, stroking her inner walls, drawing out the orgasm I can feel building.

"Fuck Madison, you are perfect."

With my free hand, I hook her leg over my shoulder. When she settles her weight on me, I reach up to pinch at her nipple again.

"Please," she begs.

"I want to feel you come on my fingers before you come on my cock."

I add another finger, hooking them inside her.

Pumping in and out. I suck and bite at her clit as she climaxes. Her walls tighten around me, legs shuddering as she rides my face through the high.

I lap at her pussy, soaking in every tiny shudder.

"Please fuck me now professor."

Placing her leg back down, I bite at her thigh. "Bedroom. Condom."

"I'm on the pill."

Her words rush through me. Blood pumps into my already aching length. Fuck the condom, I want to feel her wet pussy on my cock.

I stand, grabbing her cheeks to kiss her.

"Are you sure?"

She nods, and I lose myself to the frenzy.

Tugging my pants down, I spin her to face the wall. I grab at the globes of her ass, massaging them as I push into her. The feeling of her pussy wrapped around my bare cock, knowing how she feels, how we both feel, is enough to bring me to the edge. I pause, thinking of anything other than how perfectly we fit together as I attempt to gain a tiny sliver of composure. Her body presses back on mine, taking control. For a moment I let her use me for her pleasure.

When I take over, slamming into her, she screams.

"Fuck, yes."

I reach around her to pinch at her clit. The pressure has her coming again. Her walls contract around me and I thrust into her furiously as my balls draw up. I follow her over the edge with a burst of uncontrollable light.

It feels strange, packing up my office. Stranger still that Madison is at my side, helping to load framed certificates and office supplies into a cardboard box.

"You don't have to help."

She turns to face me from the other side of the desk. "I know, I want to."

Waking up yesterday morning, I never imagined the day would end how it did. But I'm grateful for the unexpected turn of events. Even if it means I'll never teach again, I'm not sad about that loss.

Madison and I spent the afternoon in bliss, worshipping the way our bodies fit together. It wasn't until my phone rang that we were shocked into the reality of the situation. I'd just left my job, with nothing but a verbal offer of another one from Mateo.

Professor Dausset had called to say I was expected in her office first thing this morning. That conversation was about as awkward as to be expected. She was adamant that I was fired, I maintained that I quit, and neither of us were willing to back down.

It was Madison that stepped in, in the end, surprising us both. She managed to convince Dausset to allow me to terminate the contract. Something about how damaging it would be for the university if word got out about our relationship.

I stood in awe as she fought for me. Fought for us.

There's still a lot for us to figure out, but we can do it together now.

Madison reaches into a lower cabinet, searching for anything I might want to take with me. Stepping around the desk, I hover my body over hers, pressing my weight against her behind. My hands wrap around her waist to hold her up as I push my cock against her ass.

"Can you not wait until we are home?" She giggles when she reaches a hand between us to run her palm along my rapidly growing erection.

"No."

"Okay professor." Pushing me back with a smirk, she strides away. First to the door, where she clicks the handle shut and twists the lock. Then, with a seductive sway to her steps, she moves to the window to twist the blinds closed.

Turns out I'm going to fuck her over this desk after all.

OLIVER

6 years later

Under the setting Sicilian sun, Madison looks just as beautiful as the day I met her. Probably more, considering the overwhelmed, sobbing state she had been in that day. Her golden hair reflects the sunlight. She sweeps it over her shoulder as she looks out at the sweeping vineyards of the winery.

After two years of marriage, I'm still deeply in love with my wife. If anything, I love her even more now than I did back then. But since then, we've grown together. Our lives have changed drastically, but nothing could ever smother the fire that still burns between us.

"We should write about this," she muses from the balcony. "About having to wait two years to have a honeymoon."

Madison could write about anything and sell a million copies. After she finished her degree, Madison focused all her energy on becoming the published writer she always dreamed about being. Her first novel—a romance set right here in Sicily—blew up, selling thousands of copies and gaining attention all over the world. The publisher was unsure about her second. The creative non-fiction style broke all the rules of her genre, but they gave it a chance and it too exceeded all expectations.

After that, they stopped questioning her stories. Sending off her fifth manuscript just days before we left for our honeymoon, we weren't supposed to talk about work while we were here. It was meant to be a time for just us. No agents, no editors, no laptops. But we've never been good at sticking to the rules we make for ourselves.

Between her regular releases and my infrequent ones, we've become global writing superstars. If that's even a thing. We built a brand as authors who fell in love, and I think she is right. Readers have been begging us to write collaboratively for a while now, but we never had the right story to tell. This might be it though. My thoughts swirl with the possibilities, wondering how far back in our relationship we should go. How much of our unconventional start we should tell.

I step out onto the balcony and wrap my arms around her. As I always do when we are close, I feel home.

"We should."

We watch as the sun sets, blissfully ignoring the flight we have to take home tomorrow. Our actual honeymoon might be over, but even after all these years, nothing could drag us out of the honeymoon phase.

"You're feeling better?" I ask as I open a bottle of local wine and pour us each a glass.

Earlier in our trip, the Italian food had disagreed

with her. She felt sick for weeks, but the stomach bug has finally settled.

"Yeah."

Looking down at her wine, her gentle smile shifts into a thin line. Her eyes widen as she pushes the glass into my hands. She pulls her lower lip between her teeth, frantically counting at her fingers. My cheek puffs with air as I wait for her to let me in on whatever it is that has her so excited.

Her arms hug her stomach, eyes sparkling in the dying light. Looking up, her mouth spreads back into a smile.

"I think I know what it was."

Read on for a sneak peek of

Because of Her

CASSIDY

Arriving home, I slam the door behind me as hard as I can and dump my bag so it lands on the floor with a thud. Following suit, I sink to the ground and bang my head against the wall behind me.

"Argh." I moan, as loud as possible, banging my head again for dramatic effect.

When my flatmate Amira doesn't call out with sympathy, I kick off my shoes, allowing them to clunk into the wall on the other side of the hallway. I wince, thinking about the damage I might have caused. To the shoes, not the wall. They're nothing fancy, but they are my favourite pair of boots and with the winter season coming, I can't afford to replace them.

"Aaargh." I try again, with more force this time. I'm mopey, and I know it. But if there is one person I can act like a spoiled brat around, it's Amira. I really, *really,* wanted my date with Mike to go well. There had been so much promise, and it feels like a kick straight to the kidney for it to have gone so bad.

"I'm not coming down there for you to bitch about your date, you can come here," Amira calls out from our open plan kitchen-slash-dining-slash-living area.

I crawl my way along the hallway then reach up to pull myself onto the couch.

"That bad?" Amira asks as she sits down next to me and pulls my feet into her lap.

She's still in her pyjamas, her own legs wrapped underneath the oversized sleep tee. Her long brown hair is tied into a braid that rests over her shoulder, and although her eyes are always dark, there's a shadow about them today. She'd been out to dinner with her parents last night, coming home late. She was still asleep when I left this morning, but I know how draining conversations with her father were for her.

"Did I tell you I turned down a job for this date?" I sigh.

As a florist who specialises in weddings, Saturdays are a valuable trade. Especially now, as the wedding season nears its end. It was insane, and a little concerning, that I had today off in the first place to be able to make plans. And when a last-minute opportunity came up to help another florist, saying no had been a difficult decision. I had really thought things with Mike would go well, and after my string of bad dating luck since returning to Melbourne, I couldn't turn down the one guy I actually thought had potential.

"Why were you so keen on him anyway?"

I pause, because in truth, I don't really know the answer. Sure, we got along well enough while we were chatting online, but we didn't share a heap of interests or have the same life goal. There was nothing special about Mike besides his stance on children.

I wanted it to go well like I want anything to go well.

I want someone to call after a stressful day, I want someone to snuggle up to on cold winter nights. But most of all I want someone to buy me flowers for a change. It feels ridiculous to be so hung up on wanting to find love, and I'm pretty sure that the reason I can't find it is because of how hard I'm looking.

Every terrible date makes me wonder a little more about what I did to deserve ending up here. What I did to deserve the heartache, and the gut wrenching break up that followed.

Things had been going well with Blake for years. After meeting and dating at university, we moved interstate so he could follow his dream of being a national journalist. My career was flexible, so it made sense. As our relationship progressed and the hard questions became more important, we realised that our lives no longer aligned as well as we had hoped. It's not that I never wanted children. I always had a picture in my head of how my life would go, and eventually the idea of being a parent forced its way out of that image. Blake told me that he wished he could say the same, but he couldn't.

Despite his career ambitions and all the goals he was smashing in the journalism world, he couldn't picture his future without 'fathering an heir'. He had said it with a mountain of seriousness, but I couldn't help cringing at his self-righteousness.

It broke both our hearts when we realised our paths were ultimately separating. But it tore mine in two learning that after all we had been through, he valued me no more than my ability to be a mother.

Two years later, I still often wonder how he is doing. If he found someone who could give him what I couldn't. And with every failed fling and shitty date, I wonder how different my life could be if I hadn't been dealt these cards.

"I don't know," I admit. "I just feel like I should have moved on by now. Otherwise, what was the point?"

"Well for starters you wouldn't have met me." She laughs, leaning down to squeeze me in a hug.

"I just don't understand why I attract all the crazies." I sigh.

Amira quiets her laugh.

Before Mike, there was Brad. He had seemed nice until I discovered that not only did he want children one day, he wanted a whole tribe of them. That joke, about having a soccer team, he said it without a hint of sarcasm.

There was also Justin, who had a wife on the side. And Trevor, who openly told me he was gay but was trying to hide it from his very old-fashioned grandmother. It's ok though, he had said, she will die soon and then he'll be free to live how he wants. The list of terrible flings and dates went on and on.

"Maybe you're trying to fill a hole that doesn't need filling."

I give a short, dry laugh and nudge her rib cage. "What if I really do want my hole filled?"

Amira shakes her head with an eyeroll. "I was talking about the hole in your heart you filthy whore."

Pulling a pillow from behind me, I throw it at her face. I don't have a hole in my heart, I just want someone to turn to after a long day. I want someone to choose me over everything, and everyone. Forever, not just for now.

Amira and I met not long after I moved back to the city. I had returned to my parents' place, but pretty quickly knew I needed a place of my own. Only, that's not exactly affordable on a florist's income, so I started looking for a housemate.

Amira was a cousin of a friend of a friend, whose old housemate had just moved out. So, I moved in. Our apartment is a small two-bedroom unit, close enough to the city to be trendy, without being so close that we live in a high rise with rent as high as the rooftop courtyard.

Just over a year ago, we got permission to paint the hospital white walls a more homey shade of eggshell grey, and together we have started adding colour to the decor. My grandma's pink hand-knit blanket drapes the back of the couch, and the bird paintings we did at a 'Paint 'n' Sip' class take pride of place on the wall behind it. The small round dining table is surrounded by four different chairs, each its own vibrant colour. My favourite is the royal blue upholstered dining chair. Amira prefers the traditional style wooden one that she painted red.

"Maybe it's time I stopped actively trying to find a man," I admit, more to myself than to Amira, but I know she hears me when I feel her head nod.

"Just swear off men like I have?"

I snuggle into her shoulder, whispering "deal", even though I'm not so sure. Amira flitters between swearing off men and cosying up to her latest fling weekly, so I know better than to take her seriously.

We hug for a while, and I soak up Amira's warm energy. I swear it flows through the woman like the honey of her skin. When I'm feeling a little better about my miserable start to the day, I stand up and walk to the balcony. I don't know how many pleasant days we have left before winter hits, and I plan to soak in every ounce of sun I can.

I slide open the door, expecting to hear the sounds of a busy inner suburban street. Instead, the steady beeps of a truck reversing flood the apartment.

"I think our new neighbour is moving in," I announce, stepping out and hoping to catch sight of the person, or people, we are bound to cross paths with countless times from here on out.

Amira joins me on the balcony, but I shove her back inside.

"Don't make it obvious," I hiss. "Go make tea or something so it looks like we're just two women enjoying the midday sun."

She laughs at me, but walks over to the kitchen and flicks the jug on. While she grabs our favourite mugs from the drying rack next to the sink, I lean slightly over the rusted railing to see if I can spot the new resident of apartment 32.

The unit across from ours has been empty for a few months now. We suspect the owners were trying to charge too much rent, because despite hundreds of people walking through during the openings, no one came to stay. Until now. The big "FOR RENT" sign in front of the block had been taken down last weekend.

Amira comes out with two mugs of her perfectly brewed coffee. I grab one from her as she leans on the railing with me.

"See anyone yet?"

Before I can answer her, the driver's door to the rental truck opens and a man with dark scruffy hair steps out. It's not until he is standing on the footpath that I realise just how ridiculously tall he is, and I wonder if he would have to stoop to avoid the low ceilings in the communal hallways of our building. He calls out to someone in the car in front, and soon a whole family is on the sidewalk. Two young kids start to play on the retaining wall, while five adults gather and, I assume, form a plan.

"Mum, Dad, grown-up kids, grandkids?" I look to Amira.

"Or is one of them an in-law? They all have really dark hair except that guy."

She raises a finger off her bright green mug to point. We're too far away for it to identify who she is talking about, but I can tell she is referring to the man wrangling the children off the retaining wall. His dark auburn hair stands out in the sea of dark chocolate browns.

I laugh, "I wonder who's moving in."

Together, we watch as the tall one opens the rear door of the vehicle and starts lowering the tailgate. His shirt is tight against his broad shoulders and muscular back. A sleeve of tattoos spirals around his right arm. His hair has a slight wave to it, sitting messily on the nape of his neck. A glimpse of the side of his face reveals a short beard, long enough to be on purpose, but trimmed and tidy in a way his hair isn't. I can't explain why, but there is something oddly familiar about him.

"I feel like a creep," I whisper, turning to walk back inside.

Amira follows. "We can find out who has moved in later, but if it's that guy with the tatt I call dibs."

"What happened to you swearing off men?"

She cocks her eyebrow at me. "Like you weren't checking him out too."

She's right, but it's more than his muscular frame that has me intrigued. Maybe it's something about the dragon tail wrapping around his forearm. Or how the thought of him having to stoop in the hallway feels oddly familiar, bringing back memories of hiding in the storage room during my teenage job as a supermarket cashier. Whatever it is, I'm determined to work out why I can't shake the nervous tingles spreading from my fingers.

Because of Her

Cassidy

I always want what I can't have:
My business to succeed through winter.
Someone to kiss me goodnight without the pressure
to settle down and start a family.
And now, my old high school flame.

When Callum moves in across the hall, he is just as
handsome and flirtatious as I remember.

Years ago, I thought we were perfect together. But our
worlds now are far too different. Mostly because of the
other girl in his life. His daughter.

Callum

This is not the life I planned:
A broken marriage.
A bitter custody battle.
And an undeniable attraction to the woman I
shouldn't want.

Cassidy is a ghost from my past. A reminder of the old
me. The one who was carefree and thought the best of
people, instead of the worst.

And I can't shake the feeling that our lives have been
thrown back together for a reason.
I just need to convince her that we'll work this time.

Because of Her is a steamy romance about
friendship, love and accepting the unexpected. A
standalone story, it is the first full length novel in
Bookstagrammer Devon May's Because of Love series.

Because of Her will be released on April 12th 2024.

Pre-order your copy now.

AUSTRALIA

https://www.amazon.com.au/dp/B0CR1D8LPG

USA

https://www.amazon.com/dp/B0CR1D8LPG

Acknowledgements

This one feels special for a whole host of reasons, but mainly because it's the first. It's a crazy, surreal feeling to put your work out there for the world to read, and I hope you loved Oliver and Madison as much as I do. For now at least, they are my favourites.

I wouldn't be writing this if it wasn't for the immense outpouring of support from every bookish bestie I've made over the past couple of years. Thank you for all the love and encouragement.

Especially thank you to:

Ashleigh Van Arkkels, the ultimate hype woman, editor, and all-round incredible human being.

Sarah Walker, if it wasn't for you kicking my butt, I never would have got this one out into the world.

Emma Mugglestone, for not only putting up with my endless questions, but for also planting the seed for this story.

And Shannon. Even though you said you didn't need to be thanked, I'm doing it anyway. Here's to all the nights we spent back to back in the study, you gaming and me writing.

About the Author

When she was 10, Santa brought Devon a "how to write a book" journal. Publishing her debut novel more than 20 years later, she's glad it finally got put to good use.

Devon May resides in Melbourne, Australia with her husband and the two tiny humans who call her mum. When she isn't breaking up fights, she enjoys books that either break her heart, or turn her on. She carries her emotional support Kindle everywhere, drinks far too much coffee and will never be caught without a hair tie on her wrist.

Find her on Instagram @booksbydevonmay
or join her in her Facebook group:
DM me - Devon May's Readers